Third Time's The Charm

Samantha Baca

Just One Time

Second Chances

Third Time's The Charm

Four-ever Single

Fifth Wheel

Cover Design: Richard Baca
Image(s): DepositPhotos

Contents

Contents

One
Capshaw

"Do you have the report from last week?" I asked my mom, moving around the small office space that looked like it exploded with papers.

"Umm, I think it's over there." She tapped her chin with her finger as she looked for it. "Or maybe I put it in that pile? I really have no idea."

"Mom," I sighed. "You need to hire someone to help out around here."

"I know. I will when I can find the time."

I sat on the edge of the desk and folded my hands in my lap, taking in the dark circles beneath her eyes.

"I understand it's been hard with dad having his surgery and not being able to work right now, but you're not doing him any favors by working yourself this hard."

"What am I supposed to do? Let the restaurant that we started together go under? I can't do that, Jack."

The emotion in her voice tugged at my heart, making me hate that there wasn't more that I could do. Add in that she'd called me *Jack* and not *Capshaw*, and I felt even more like a mama's boy than normal. I had been a firefighter for so long that everyone around town called me by my last name, including my family. My mom was the only one who ever called me Jack anymore, and it usually only happened when she was upset, which made this even worse.

But I understood where she was coming from and how much Surf 'N Shack meant to her. Hell, to all of us. My mom first met my stepdad, Phil, shortly after my dad walked out and left us when I was ten years old. He stepped in and took me in as his child and built a life for us we could never have imagined before. Shortly after they got married, they opened Surf 'N Shack, and it's been our family business ever since.

"I have a solution to your problem," my sister Lia said, entering the already crammed office.

"I'd love to hear this," I said, scrubbing my hand down the scruff that dotted my jawline.

She narrowed her eyes at me and then smiled at our mom, reaching in to hug her as she stuck her tongue out at me over her shoulder.

"Hey, baby," my mom replied, cupping the sides of my sister's face between her hands. "Let's hear what you have for us."

"Well, I have a friend who is in between jobs right now and—"

"No," I interrupted, cutting off her sentence.

"You didn't even let me finish."

"I don't need to. We need someone who is reliable, Lia. Not some bratty kid who doesn't know the value of working and has no respect."

"Why is that the first thing you go to?" She planted her hands on her hips and glared at me.

"Because I remember the handful of *friends* you've referred along the way, Lia. We don't need a bunch of frat guys in here, too busy checking out the girls to be helpful."

"Well, lucky for you, *she's* not a frat guy."

A flash of fiery red hair caught my eye, and I immediately knew who was standing outside the door, though it had been years since I last saw her.

"Come on in, Kens. They won't bite."

The kitchen was quieter than usual, which made me think the guys were all too busy staring at Lia's friend instead of working.

"Get back to work," I yelled, my voice booming through the small office space. Suddenly, the noise level returned to normal as the guys got focused again.

"Oh, Kensy dear," my mother exclaimed, rushing over to hug her as soon as she stepped inside. "It's so good to see you!"

"You just saw her yesterday, mom," Lia laughed, shaking her head and rolling her eyes.

"I know, but I've missed her so much!"

"*This* is who you're referring to," I asked my sister, my voice low as I studied Kensy.

She'd been my sister's best friend for years, so I was very familiar with who she was. A few years ago, Kensy moved to Texas with her father but kept in touch with Lia while she was gone. I'd heard that she moved back to town after her father passed away, but no one bothered to mention that she looked more like a damn woman now and not the goofy teenager she left as.

"Yes. She needs a job, and we need help."

I closed my eyes and sighed heavily.

"Lia, we need actual help. Someone who can run the register, clean tables, and help in the kitchen. Someone who isn't afraid to get their hands dirty." I didn't mean to sound so condescending, but I also couldn't picture myself working with Kensy every day and *not* thinking about her in a way I shouldn't. It would be better for everyone if we found someone else. *Anyone* else.

"You're so judgmental," she laughed. "You sure get crotchetier the older you get. I'd hate to see how you are when you turn forty—though that's only a few years away, so I guess I don't have to wait too long."

"Shut up, I'm only thirty-six. And I'm not crotchety, Lia. I'm looking out for our family business which can't afford to hire people just for fun right now. We need someone who is going to come in and bust their ass every day."

"I know," she said heavily while my mom and Kensy continued talking. "But she really, really needs this job. She won't screw it up, I promise."

I worked my jaw back and forth, trying to come up with another reason why Kensy wouldn't be a good fit for Surf 'N Shack but came up empty.

"Besides, it's not like you even have to worry about it," Lia added. "You can go back to the firehouse and trust that things will be okay here."

I swallowed hard, trying to push back the lump in my throat as emerald green eyes locked onto mine.

"I'm not going back for a few weeks. Maybe longer."

"What? Since when?" Lia asked, her voice loud enough to draw my mom's attention to our conversation.

"Since last week. I'm on indefinite leave."

My mom covered her mouth and gasped.

"Son, you didn't have to do that," she whispered.

I inhaled deeply, feeling the pull in my lungs before I let it out.

"I know. I wanted to." I shrugged, hoping it would stop the sympathetic looks I was receiving from everyone in the room.

"I didn't want our troubles to become yours." My mom sat down in the chair in the corner and shook her head. Lia stood next to her and squeezed her shoulders in a hug.

"They're not just your problems, Mom. They're all of ours. This is *our* family business, and I'm not going to walk away when you need me. This is just a small bump. We'll get over it and be back to normal again." I spoke the words but had a hard time ignoring the feeling in my gut, saying they might have been a lie.

"If we all pitch in, we can do this," Lia added, reaching down to hold my mom's hand. "I'll pick up some shifts between classes and cover the weekends."

"I know the job isn't mine yet, but I have availability during the week, which is when Lia said you guys needed someone," Kensy said, looking sheepishly at me before lowering her eyes.

"What kind of experience do you have?" I asked her, folding my arms over my chest.

"I waitressed at a pizza parlor for a few years in Texas, and then after that, I bartended for six months before moving back last week."

I rolled my neck on my shoulders and sighed heavily. I saw the looks on my mom and Lia's face as they practically begged me to give in and offer her the job. It wasn't technically my place to hire or fire people, but my mom was too much of a softie to handle any of that, so I'd taken over for my dad while he was out recovering.

"When can you start?"

The sound of women squealing and shrieking excitedly drowned out whatever answer Kensy might have given.

<u>Two</u>
Kensy

"I can't believe I got the job!" I shrieked, linking my arm into Lia's as we left Surf 'N Shack and headed to her studio apartment, where I was currently staying until I could get on my feet.

"I told you that you would," she laughed.

"Yeah, but your brother is a lot scarier than he used to be. And when did he get so tall? And muscular? Not to mention that strong jawline. Was that always there, or did I miss it?"

Lia stopped walking and stared at me.

"Are you into my brother?" she asked, no hint of amusement in her now icy blue eyes.

I pulled my head back, trying to hide the embarrassment washing over me. *Was I into Jack?*

"No. Not at all." I laughed to try to shake off the nerves that were still washing over me. "I just didn't realize how much he's changed since the last time I saw him. That's all."

She studied me for a few minutes as my heart beat wildly in my chest.

"Alright," she said, though she didn't sound like she bought any of the lies I just tried to feed her. "Let's get to Tipsy

Taquito before they run out of happy hour margaritas."

"Tipsy Taquito?" I questioned, knowing that the plan was to go back to her place and eat Ramen noodles.

"To celebrate," she said with a shrug before a huge smile split her cheeks.

I followed her to her car and got in, still trying to fight the butterflies swarming in my stomach from seeing her brother. Surely that was just because it had been so long since I had seen him and would pass, right?

By Monday morning, it had been three days since I'd seen him, and I was even more of a mess for my first day at work than I'd expected. On top of that, Lia told me that I would report to him when I got there, which meant that we would spend the entire day together while he taught me the ropes.

I ran a brush through my hair once more and then fastened a hair tie around it, pulling it up into a high ponytail. I'd gone with minimal makeup, a touch of lipstick and some mascara, so I didn't look like death from the lack of sleep I got last night.

Not only was the couch at Lia's not comfortable, but my mind also wouldn't stop racing. After we got back from happy hour the other night, I'd spent a few hours on my phone, looking him up on social media. I was surprised by some of the photos he'd used as his profile picture with him wearing his firefighter gear. He looked delicious and I hated that I was allowing myself to think that way about him after Lia had made it abundantly clear that he was off-limits to me.

I might have stared at his pictures for so long that I had memorized the tiny mole above his right eyebrow and how it was hidden in some photos. His hair hung over it in a sexy, mused-up way when it wasn't cut short and faded in the back like it was when I saw him the other day.

But the one thing that was consistent in all the pictures was his dark blue eyes which reminded me of the ocean. I wanted to get lost in their depths and go deep sea diving—which meant a lot for someone like me who was terrified of the open water and sharks. But still, I would be willing to brave getting eaten by a shark just to spend some time staring into those beautiful eyes—especially if that shark's name was Jack.

I shook my head, forcing the daydreams of him away as I took one last look in the mirror before heading to work. It still felt weird to say that, but I refused to think too much about it. I was lucky that Lia was able to get me this job, now I just had to do my best not to lose it.

By the time I got to the Surf 'N Shack, I was sweaty from riding the bus that had no air conditioning in the middle of summer. I'd worn jeans and a t-shirt, unsure of what was an appropriate dress code given I was too distracted when I'd gone in with Lia to notice what everyone else was wearing.

Thanks to my long torso, I tugged at the bottom of my shirt to keep it from riding up and pulled the handle to open the door. I sucked in a deep breath and pulled my shoulders back. It was showtime.

The restaurant was relatively quiet, probably because it was only eleven o'clock in the morning, and their lunch rush didn't start until noon. They only served lunch and dinner, which meant that my shifts in the morning would start before everyone else got there and that I would be helping Jack with some of the prep work.

I waved at the woman wiping down the tables as I stepped inside and nervously looked around.

"He's in the office," she said, already knowing who I was looking for.

"Thank you." I adjusted my purse on my shoulder and headed that way when I spotted him coming out.

"Good morning," I stammered, those pesky butterflies taking flight in my stomach again.

"Hey. Go ahead and put your purse in the office, and then I'll show you around."

I did as he asked, then joined him in the kitchen, where he was talking to a few of the guys at the stove.

"We have a large party coming in tonight, so you need to make sure we have enough shrimp and catfish. Plan accordingly throughout the day and 86 it if you guys run short. I do not want anyone getting into the reserve that I've set aside, got it?"

They both nodded and then looked at me, making Jack turn in my direction.

"Guys, this is Kensy. Kensy, this is Leon and Frankie. They've been with us for years and know the ins and outs of the restaurant. They're your best resources if you need anything and I'm not around."

"Sounds good. Nice to meet you guys." I smiled and tugged nervously at my ear, looking for a strand of hair to twirl.

The rest of the morning passed by quickly as he showed me around and gave me the rundown of what I would be responsible for doing every day. While I was more relaxed about the job in general, I couldn't deny the sparks I felt between us every time our bodies accidentally brushed against each other. But I was here to do a job, and that didn't entail riding Jack on the counter while ringing up customers.

12

Three
Capshaw

Getting Kensy set up this morning was easier than I had anticipated, though it definitely helped that she had previous experience working at the pizza parlor in Texas. I spent twenty minutes showing her how to use the register once our lunch rush started, then had to run off to handle a kitchen fire. By the time I got back, she had the line moving smoothly and looked like a pro who had been doing this for years.

"Sorry about that," I said quietly as I stood beside her and smiled at the customers in line.

"Not a problem at all. The lady over in the corner asked to speak to a manager, so I told her you'd be with her as soon as you were available." She spoke out of the side of her mouth as she nodded, taking the customer's order and entering it in.

I looked over to where she had indicated and found Mrs. Dawson waiting for me. Without thinking, I gently slid my hand across her lower back and slid out behind the register to go speak to her. Her body tensed slightly in reaction before I pulled away.

I talked with Mrs. Dawson for a few minutes, confirming that we would be happy to host her husband's retirement party next month. I gave her my business card and asked that she call me when she had the details of how many people they would be expecting and what they would like on the menu.

After she left, I stood back for a few minutes and watched Kensy as her head tipped back slightly to laugh at something Mr. Bucky had said. He was one of the sweetest people in town and didn't miss his daily fish and chips, even though his doctor advised him to make it every other day. In his words— tomorrow is never expected, so why risk *not* getting them, just in case that's the day he gets called home?

The line continued to move smoothly, and I felt some of the initial trepidation about hiring her start to wear off. I knew that Kensy was a good girl from when she used to hang out with Lia, but that was years ago. She was twenty-five now, and I remembered how wild and reckless I had been at that age, so I couldn't help but wonder if she wasn't the same. But seeing her putting in the effort to get the job done made me wonder if maybe I'd been wrong about her all along. Maybe Kensy had grown up and matured into the beautiful woman who was now locking eyes with me from across the room.

Her red lips turned up into a smile before she looked away and gave her attention to the customer in front of her while I headed back to my office to deal with the situation that was now happening in my pants.

The afternoon was busy and ended up with me on the line cooking while Kensy handled the register. It was amazing how seamlessly everything went. Other than the one small kitchen fire, there were no other issues, and I felt more relaxed than I had in a few weeks.

By 3:30, I was up front, getting ready for the dinner rush, when Kensy came over and joined me. Without saying a word, she sat down and grabbed a handful of napkins before wrapping utensils.

We worked quietly, neither of us saying anything but being equally aware of each other as our hands brushed when we both reached for forks at the same time. She pulled away quickly, a burst of color flushing her fair cheeks.

"Sorry," she whispered.

"Don't be." I rubbed my lips together to keep from saying anything more.

Suddenly, her phone started ringing, and her eyes widened with fear.

She pulled her eyebrows together as she scrambled to pull it out and silence it.

"I'm—"

"Kensy, it's okay. Answer the call. We're not busy, and you didn't take a break earlier. Use this time now and take your phone call." I nodded to the phone that was still ringing in her hand.

"Are you sure?" Her brows were still furrowed as she stood up and clutched it to her chest.

I nodded and slowly inhaled as she stood up, her tropical-scented perfume floating in the air around us. She walked off, her hips swaying as her jeans wrapped snuggly around her firm ass. I forced myself to look away and stop checking her out.

A few minutes later, she returned, tucking her phone into her pocket before sitting down and wrapping more silverware.

"I'm so sorry about that. I thought it was on silent, and that was a potential client that Lia was trying to set up for me."

"Client?" I asked, feeling my jaw tighten slightly as I wondered what kind of work she was doing where she had *clients*. My mind immediately went in the wrong direction, and I hated myself for hoping maybe *I* could be her *client*.

"I do photography," she explained, looking up at me briefly under her dark lashes. "I'm trying to get set up in town to do some family sessions, and Lia said she knew someone who might be interested. I guess it's a former coworker of yours. Nate Wilson?"

I nodded and tossed the wrapped silverware I'd finished onto the pile.

"Yeah, he was my captain. Is my captain? I guess I'm not sure what to call him anymore." I hated the uncertainty in my voice, not knowing what the future held for me and if I would ever go back to being a firefighter again.

Her face fell as if she could sense the emotions washing over me.

"Nate's a great guy," I said, shifting the conversation. "He and his wife just had their second baby."

"That's what Lia was telling me. I spoke with Abby, and she said they'd be interested in doing some family photos, but she wanted to see if her sister, Jane, might want to do some as well."

I skipped past the part about my history with Jane and offered her a smile instead.

"That sounds like a great place to start. There are a lot of families expecting babies around here, so you should be able to get the ball rolling pretty easily."

"Wow, it sounds like something's in the water," she joked.

"Yeah, that's why I stick with whiskey." I winked, not

meaning to come on so strong, but the way she looked at me made me want to do it again.

"I guess maybe I should stick to whiskey too. I mean, not that there's anything to worry about since I'm not dating anyone. But, you know, if you're ever looking for a whiskey-drinking partner, I'm your girl."

So many thoughts rushed through my head, all begging for my attention. My mom chose that moment to walk in and grin foolishly as soon as she spotted us together at the table.

"Hey, Mom," I said, standing up and pushing my chair in. It felt like I'd been caught doing something I shouldn't, and I hated that feeling. But I hadn't done anything wrong other than entertain thoughts about my little sister's best friend that I shouldn't.

"Hey, Jack. How are things going today? How's your first day, Kensy?"

She looked between us, and her eyes lit up in a way I hadn't seen in forever.

"It's been wonderful. Thank you, Mrs. Capshaw."

Kensy stood up and wrapped my mom in a hug.

"Oh, please, call me Maria. Mrs. Capshaw makes me feel old," she joked, swatting her arm playfully.

"Thank you again for this opportunity, Maria. I'm very grateful to have found employment so quickly."

"Well, you're like family, my dear. We take care of each other, and that includes you."

I swallowed hard, trying not to think about the words trying to impregnate themselves in my head. *We're like family.* She wasn't technically related to us, but that didn't mean that the rest of my family didn't see her as such.

"I need to get to the back and check on things before the dinner rush," I blurted out, giving my mom a quick peck on the cheek before rushing off and leaving her there to talk to Kensy.

Four
Kensy

"How was your first day?" Lia asked as soon as I walked in and closed the door behind me. It wasn't hard to find her given that her studio apartment was tiny and everything was in the same small space.

"It was good," I sighed, taking my purse off and hanging it on the coat rack by the door. "Really good."

"I heard there was a fire." She lifted the spatula from the pan and raised her eyebrows.

"There was, but it wasn't my fault. It was a small grease fire, and your brother immediately took care of it."

"He better have; he is a firefighter," she laughed. "I'm making cheeseburger hamburger helper for dinner. Grab a plate, and I'll load you up."

"Thanks." I grabbed one of the paper plates from the stack in the corner of the counter and held it in front of her. Lia hated to do dishes—something I learned quickly the first night I stayed with her.

Between working a full-time job, helping at her parent's restaurant, and going to med school, she didn't have much time for anything fun, which meant she wasn't going to waste a single second of what time she did have, doing dishes.

I took my plate, grabbed a fork, and sat on the couch that also doubled as a dining room table, given that she didn't have space for one. It was also currently my bed until I could get on my feet and afford to buy one. Lia had a bed, but it was small and barely fit in the corner of the living room, so it wasn't like we could share it.

A few minutes later, she joined me and we ate dinner while watching reruns on TV. It was a simple meal shared with my best friend, making it one of the best meals I'd had in a long time.

After dinner, we hung out for a while, mainly just sitting on the couch and playing on our phones. I was busy looking for apartments while she was doing something that had a grin pulling tightly across her face.

I knew that she had a different dad than Jack, but they definitely got their piercing blue eyes from their mom. Hers were wide as her fingers rushed across the screen, typing something as she chewed her lip.

"Who are you flirting with?" I asked, lowering my phone so I could see her.

"What?" she replied, looking guilty as a blush crept up her neck. "I'm not flirting with anyone."

"Bullshit."

"I'm not!" She laughed nervously, her phone dinging with another text message that immediately grabbed her attention.

Whether or not she realized she was doing it, her smile grew even larger, and I was worried it would start hurting.

"Ahem," I said, clearing my throat once she was done typing whatever it was before she pressed send.

"Okay, okay." She giggled. "I've been talking to this guy in my pharmacology class. He wants to set up a study session before our test next week."

"Is he cute?" I asked, my smile now matching hers.

She nodded and held her phone to her chest.

"So fucking hot! I mean, I couldn't imagine having to be one of his patients. I'd probably have a heart attack from how smoking hot he is. But then again, maybe that wouldn't be such a bad thing because at least he'd have to do CPR on me."

I laughed, loving how happy she was.

"When are you guys supposed to get together?"

"I don't know," she sighed, looking down at her phone again. "We're trying to figure that out."

I looked down at my phone, noticing it was barely after 6:30, and wondered if she wasn't inviting him over because I was there.

"Well, I'm going to go out for a bit and look for spots to do some of the family sessions," I said, hoping she would pick up on what I was saying. "I'm sure I'll be out for a while. I have some shopping to do, too."

That was a lie, especially since I didn't have anywhere to store anything. I didn't have a car, and everything that I brought with me from Texas was currently crammed into the tiniest storage unit I could find and afford until I could get on my feet. I didn't have the luxury to buy anything that wasn't a necessity, but she didn't need to know that.

"Oh," she replied, pulling her head back as she thought about it. "Are you sure?"

"Yeah, I actually talked with Abby today, and she's interested in setting up a session. She thinks her sister might want to as well, so I need to go look at different options and get used to where the good spots are in Beaumont Creek."

I got up and grabbed my flip-flops, thankful that I had changed into shorts as soon as I got home.

"You don't have to do that," she said, suddenly scowling at me.

"Do what?" I looked up at her as I bent over and grabbed my purse.

"Leave."

"I know. But I do need to start looking at places if I want to try to get my photography business going. It's not going to do me any favors if I don't have recommendations on the best places to go to capture the photos people will want."

"But tonight? It feels like you're doing this just so I can invite Joseph over to study."

"Nope," I lied. "It's just a coincidence. I'm supposed to meet with Abby this weekend, so I can't just sit on my ass all week."

"Are you sure?"

"Positive. I'll be back in a little bit, but I'll text when I'm on my way. Just in case you need something."

"Alright," she sighed. "But please don't feel like you have to be out all night. You can be here while we study."

I scrunched my nose.

"What?" She laughed and raised her shoulders.

"I don't want to be here while you guys talk about body parts," I teased. "Nor do I want to see any if I walk in on something."

"You're not going to walk in on anything," she assured me with a cheeky grin.

"I've heard that before." I slung my purse over my shoulder and pinned her with a look.

"That was *one* time, Kensy. One time!"

I planted my hand on my hip and waited for her memories to catch up.

"Okay, twice."

"Shit, three times."

Her face turned redder as she realized how many times it had really been.

"Alright," she conceded. "Point taken."

I laughed and shook my head.

"I'll text when I'm headed back. Just use *syphilis* as a code word if you need me to give you more time."

"Really? Syphilis?"

"What? Do you prefer chlamydia? Gonorrhea? What's your disease of choice?"

"You're terrible," she said, trying to hide her laughter.

"But you love me." I winked at her over my shoulder before I left.

24

<u>Five</u>
Capshaw

"So, when are you coming back?" Rodriguez asked, leaning against the counter as I rang up his order. It was the fifth time my old platoon had stopped by for food this week, which wasn't completely out of the norm, but they also hadn't given up on asking me when I was planning to return.

"I don't know," I sighed heavily. "Things with my dad are still up in the air, so until we know when he can come back to work, I'll be here helping out."

"But you are coming back, right?"

I smiled at Jones, hearing the sadness in his voice. He was still the rookie, given we hadn't brought anyone else on since he joined us almost two years ago, and I had taken him under my wing and tried to teach him the ropes when he wasn't accidentally setting the kitchen on fire every chance he got.

"That's the plan." I turned my attention to Nate and knew that I could count on him to change the topic. "So, how did Penny like the hushpuppies? Did Abby get any?"

"She loved them so much that she ate all of them—including the ones I got for Abby and me." He laughed, and I admired the look in his eyes when he spoke of his family. It was the same look I'd seen my stepdad have when he talked about my mom and vice versa, though it wasn't anything I'd ever experienced on my own.

"I'll make sure to throw in some extra for you today," I chuckled as I finished inputting his order.

"Thank you, just don't tell Abby," he joked, handing me his credit card.

"Your secret is safe with me, but if she comes in with that cake…." I raised my eyebrows.

"I'll be sure to ask Sherry to hide the ingredients and keep Abby there today."

I laughed and handed his card back to him.

"And here I was thinking I was going to get some cake today."

"Is it your birthday?" Kensy asked, coming up beside me and making me jump. She smiled at the guys and then locked eyes with me while she waited.

"No," I coughed out, suddenly feeling like I'd been caught doing something even though I hadn't. I knew the guys would give me shit for how I just reacted with her, but there was no way to deny my body's response whenever she was around. Trust me—I'd been trying for over a week, ever since she walked in her first day.

"Oh," she replied with a confused frown. "Do you want cake? I'm not a professional baker or anything, but I can try to whip one up now that it's slowing down some."

"That's okay, but thank you."

The guys were watching us intently, several smirks playing across their faces.

"It's a special cake that my wife makes," Nate offered, refusing to meet the glare I gave him.

"What kind of cake is it?" Kensy asked, leaning closer to me to hear Nate as her breasts slightly grazed the back of my arm.

"They call it the *sex cake*," Jones said, too young to have a solid filter on him.

Kensy's eyes widened, and I felt her step away from me as if the word *sex* shouldn't be said while we were standing so close to each other.

"Why do they call it that?" she asked, her voice barely above a whisper.

"Because," Nate said slowly, looking from her to me. "Someone once said that it was better than sex. After that, everyone just started calling it the *sex cake*."

Time felt like it was moving painfully slowly as Kensy's jaw dropped, and the guys grinned even wider.

"Oh my," she finally replied. "I better go check on those to-go orders."

She turned and walked away, allowing me the chance to finally let out the breath I had been holding so I didn't have to inhale the intoxicating scent of her perfume. I avoided looking at the guys as I rubbed my hand down my face, feeling the course scruff that dotted my jawline.

"Now I see why you're not in a hurry to come back," Rodriguez joked, ducking when I tossed a crumpled-up piece of paper at his head.

"Shut up. It's not like that."

"Like what?" Nate asked, his smirk matching the others.

"She's my sister's best friend."

"And?" Rodriguez pushed, joining forces with Nate.

"She's off limits."

I got the words out right before she came back, though I couldn't tell if she'd heard them or not. Honestly, it didn't matter. At the end of the day, she was off limits, and it was better for everyone if we remembered that.

<u>Six</u>
Kensy

"Are you ready yet?" I hollered to Lia as she finished up in the bathroom. "I'm starving…."

"Sorry, it takes a lot of work to look this good." She winked to let me know she was kidding, then dramatically rubbed her hands down her body.

"Oh, please. You're naturally beautiful, and you know it. I, on the other hand, am going to turn into an ugly, red monster if you don't hurry your ass up so we can go eat."

"Calm your tits; I'm ready. Plus, it's not like Tipsy Taquito is going to run out of food."

"No, but it's Friday night, and they're going to be busy. I want to get a booth in the back where I can hide in the shadows and stuff my face with chips and guacamole."

I lifted my hands and gave her a visual as I closed my eyes and pretended to shove food into my mouth.

"You're so fucking hot," she said dryly, shoving the lip gloss tube into her purse. "How are you still single?"

"It's simple." I shrugged. "Guys just can't handle my love for all things salty."

Her eyes widened as she clasped her hands over her mouth to hide her laughter. I'd realized what I said as soon as I said it, but she was going to make sure I heard it again.

"Oh, I'm sure plenty of guys could handle your love for *all things salty*. Again, how are you single?"

"Shut up," I laughed, smacking her arm as I grabbed my wallet and pushed past her. "Just for that, I'm having an extra margarita, and you're stuck driving us tonight."

"Alright," she said. "Might as well get it with extra salt on the rim."

By the time we got to Tipsy Taquito, there was already a line out the door. I frowned and leaned to the side, hoping that I could will people to move out of the way if I tried hard enough. When we continued to be stuck in the same spot for a few minutes, I realized I didn't have any Jedi mind tricks and gave up.

"Do you want to go somewhere else?" I asked, full on disappointment thick in my voice. "This is going to take forever."

"By the time we leave and go somewhere else, the line will have cleared, and you could be drinking your margarita. It'll go quickly, trust me."

I let her pull me into her side and hug me as I tried to push my grumpy mood away. I was just hungry and would feel better once I got some food in me. Lia's phone rang, so she pulled it out of her pocket and answered it as the line started moving.

Soon, we were inside, the heavenly smell of food permeating the air around us as music thumped in the speakers above. According to Lia, Friday nights were always busy at Tipsy Taquito because it was one of the few places in town that felt like a bar with loud music and ninety-nine cent tacos. On top of that, they had great drink prices and margaritas that were top-notch.

Lia plugged her ear with one finger while holding her phone to the other, trying to hear what was being said. I scanned the crowd, people watching as I waited. A handful of people our age took up the long bench tables in the middle of the restaurant, next to the makeshift dance floor, where they'd moved a few tables off to the side.

I'd only been here a few times since I'd been back in town, but the food was delicious, and there was a pool table in the corner that never seemed to get much attention. I kept an eye on the empty booth that I wanted while moving forward with the line.

My stomach growled as I stepped up to the register and placed my order, making sure to order an extra side of guacamole because I didn't want to come back through the line later. Once I had my sign for the table, I pointed to the booth where I was headed while Lia finished her phone call so she could put in her order. She nodded and pointed, which I assumed was just her confirming that she would meet me there.

I had my head down as I walked, not paying attention to much around me until I got to the booth. I set the number card on the table and plopped down, closing my eyes, thankful to be this much closer to eating.

"Are you okay?" a deep voice asked, startling me.

My eyes whipped open, landing on a pair of dark blue ones watching me.

"Jack?"

His lips pulled into a crooked grin before he lifted his beer mug to his lips and took a drink.

"What are you doing here?"

"I'm meeting a friend for dinner," he answered without any explanation as to why he was sitting in front of me.

"Okay. But why are you in my booth?"

He tilted his head to the side, the grin now fully spreading to both sides of his face.

"Your booth?"

"Yes, *my* booth. I've had my eye on it from the moment we got here, and it was empty until you decided to join me a few seconds ago."

He shook his head and hid his laughter behind a closed fist as he set his mug down.

"I was actually here first. You came storming over and threw yourself into the booth without noticing me."

I narrowed my eyes at him and wondered if that was true. I was so out of it, daydreaming about my guacamole feast headed my way, that I hadn't paid attention too much.

"How long have you been sitting here?" I asked. "And where is your friend?"

He looked down at his watch.

"About five minutes, and he's in the bathroom."

"How did I miss you sitting here?"

"I don't know," he said with a laugh. "You did seem kind of distracted."

"Well, I was focused on food. Nothing else mattered at the time."

I smiled and felt butterflies rush through my stomach when he returned it.

"Sorry for not seeing you here before I just jumped in," I laughed, reaching over to grab the number sign.

His hand reached over and covered mine.

"It's fine. You should stay. There aren't any other tables open, so we can share this one."

"I'm here with Lia," I blurted out, unable to think straight with his hand still touching mine.

"Well, she can join us too."

"You bet your ass I can," Lia said as she walked up and immediately noticed our hands. Her brows pulled together, wrinkling in the middle.

Jack and I pulled away at the same time. I kept my head down, and my eyes lowered as I scooted over to make room for her. She gave me a look but I ignored it, trying not to make a scene.

"What are you doing here?" Lia asked her brother as she added her number sign with mine and Jack's on the table.

"Having dinner and stealing Kensy's booth when she wasn't looking."

"By yourself?" Lia questioned, right as a server approached with a tray of food.

"I have a taco basket with a side of guacamole," the server said, looking between us.

"That's me," Jack said, taking the number card from the sign and handing it to the guy once he got his food.

"I also have a beef taquito platter with a side of sour cream and jalapeno cream sauce."

"That one's mine."

I looked up to find one of the firefighters Jack worked with standing beside the waiter.

He collected the number for his food and then glanced at mine and Lia's before heading back to the kitchen.

"Hey, Lia, why don't you sit on this side, so Jones and I don't have to be on top of each other?" Jack asked as his friend stood at the end of the table.

"I don't want to sit by you either," Lia said, nose scrunched up.

Jack leveled her with a look that made her roll her eyes. I felt bad for stealing their table, even though I didn't technically know they were there.

"Let me out and I'll sit with Jack," I offered to Lia.

She sighed and got up, smiling at Jones as he stepped aside to make room for us.

"It's so weird to hear people call him Jack," she teased, giving me a hard time for not calling him Capshaw like everyone else. But I couldn't help it, I'd only ever known him as Jack, and that's what he would always be to me.

"*You* used to call me Jack," he countered, pointing a finger at her. "Until you thought you were too cool for your own brother."

"I've always been too cool." She stuck her tongue out at him as I slid out of the booth and maneuvered past her to get in on the other side.

Once we were all settled, the waiter returned a few minutes later with mine and Lia's food. Thankfully, everyone was too hungry to bother making small talk and dove into their dishes instead. Our margaritas arrived shortly after that, and I was in pure heaven. I had my tacos, loads and loads of guacamole, and a man I couldn't touch sitting right next to me.

"You know what's funny?" Lia said, blotting the side of her mouth with a napkin while she finished chewing her bite. "I thought my brother was the only person who was that obsessed with guacamole until now. You guys are practically twins, both eating tacos drenched in it."

I froze with my hand midair, headed toward my mouth when I looked over and saw that we basically had ordered the same thing. The only thing that was different was that he had twice as many tacos as I did and a variety where I only had chicken.

"What can I say? We know good food."

"I don't think I've ever met anyone who loves tacos as much as Capshaw does," Jones said with a laugh. "It doesn't matter what kind of taco it is—he'll eat it. Day or night, hot or cold—he loves his tacos."

I shifted uncomfortably in the booth, trying to ignore the double meaning I was getting from Jones telling us how much Jack loved tacos. I knew that he meant literal tacos, but the warm ache between my thighs was hoping that maybe there was another kind that he liked just as much.

Seven
Capshaw

The music thumped heavily against the walls, making it hard to hear whatever my sister was rambling on about. I wanted to focus on what she was saying, but it was hard with Kensy sitting right beside me, her body pulling mine closer to her with this magnetic energy that I was determined to fight.

Finally, the music stopped, and a young kid wearing hipster glasses spoke into a microphone, announcing that karaoke would be starting soon. Jones squirmed in his seat, and I couldn't tell if it was because he was nervous about the singing or if it was from sitting so close to Lia—she was known to have that effect on people and make them want to run.

I hadn't planned on sticking around tonight. It was initially supposed to be just Jones and me grabbing a bite to eat. But when I saw Lia hand Kensy a paper to fill out her song choice, I knew I wasn't going anywhere anytime soon.

Kensy tapped the pen to her chin as she thought, then scribbled something down and handed it to Lia, who reached behind her and tossed it into the basket as the DJ walked by.

"What are you going to sing?" Lia asked, looking at me while she took a drink of her margarita.

I shook my head and tried to blow it off, but this immediately caught Kensy's attention.

"You sing?" she asked enthusiastically.

"Na, not really."

"Bullshit," Lia said as she set the heavy glass on the table. "He sings all the time."

"That doesn't mean that I do karaoke."

"Yeah, and it doesn't mean that you *don't*. I've seen you do it a thousand times." Lia folded her arms over her chest. "His voice is amazing—even if it pains me to say so." She scrunched her face as if it grossed her out to think something nice about me, the joys of having a younger sister.

"Why don't you sing?" I asked, pushing the attention back to her.

"Eh, I'm not in the mood." She shrugged her shoulders and then lifted her glass for another drink.

"Maybe you and Jones could sing a song together," Kensy suggested, giving my sister a pointed look I couldn't quite figure out.

Lia narrowed her eyes at Kensy, her fingers gripping the rim of the glass so tight I worried it might break.

"I wouldn't know what to sing with someone else," Lia said through gritted teeth.

Jones looked between us, looking just as confused as I felt.

"I can sing with you," he offered quietly, turning in his seat to look at her.

A blush crept up my sister's neck, right to her cheeks, as she tried to avoid looking at me.

"Umm, okay," she whispered as Jones smiled brightly at her. "What do you want to sing?"

They flipped through the pages of the book until they found one that they both agreed on and then wrote their choice down on a paper and passed it to the DJ when he came around again. I sat there tapping my fingers to the beat as a drunk college girl belted out a Mariah Carrey song. I knew that Kensy had one song she was going to sing, as well as Lia and Jones, but since there wasn't anything I was planning to do, I got up and used the restroom.

When I came back, Lia and Jones were standing on the makeshift stage, holding microphones in their hands as they waited for the song to start. I slid into the booth next to Kensy and ignored how my body tingled as my leg touched hers.

We sat there patiently waiting for them to start, a familiar tune playing over the speakers. Soon, everyone sang along to Sweet Caroline, and the energy was contagious. I refrained from singing along, more so because I wasn't ready to let Kensy see that side of me yet. I didn't usually hold back or care what people thought about me, but she was different.

Once they were done, the audience erupted in applause while they returned to the table. The DJ reached his hand into the bowl and shuffled the names around before pulling one out and announcing the next person to sing.

"Up next, we have Jack Capshaw and Kensy Livingston singing Livin' On A Prayer by Bon Jovi!" the DJ announced.

My eyes shot up to my forehead as I looked around the table and immediately found the culprit as Lia cowered behind her glass and giggled. I glanced at Kensy, who looked just as surprised as me.

"Where you guys at?" the DJ asked, looking around the room for us.

I inhaled deeply and then let it out as I stood up and held my hand out for Kensy.

"You're so going to pay for this," I said to Lia as Kensy climbed out.

We stood in the same spot as Lia and Jones, feeling the eyes of everyone in the crowd as they stared at us. The music started, and I tried to get into the song, but it felt weird to be singing it with Kensy. We'd never sung together before, but when she started singing, I just stopped and stared at her.

Her voice was beautiful and more than I could have imagined. I was as lost by the sound as was the crowd as they hooted and hollered for her. She grinned and nudged me with her elbow, raising her eyebrows for me to join her.

I began singing, turning away from her and staring out into the crowd to keep from locking eyes with her and serenading her. But no matter how hard I tried to forget how I felt next to her, I couldn't deny the chemistry between us. So palpable that I could feel it every time we got close to each other, our bodies craving for the other's touch.

As the song progressed, I noticed some of the guys sitting at the table in front of us taking an interest in Kensy as they whistled and made inappropriate gestures. Their eyes roamed over her body, and I knew what they were thinking, which only pissed me off and made me feel more jealous than I had a right to be.

Once we were done, I headed back to the table while she excused herself to the bathroom. I sat down across from Lia and raised an eyebrow at her disapprovingly.

"What the hell was that all about?" I asked, hoping to get to the bottom of it before Kensy returned.

"What?" She laughed and held her hands up. "You love to sing. She loves to sing. I thought it would be fun for you guys to sing together. Maybe get you out of your crabby funk for a bit."

"You should have asked first."

"Why? It's just singing, Jack. Calm down."

"No, Lia, it wasn't just singing. It was—" I stopped what I was saying because I realized that I was about to admit that I was feeling something for Kensy. I hadn't even allowed myself to accept it yet, so the last thing I wanted was to discuss it with my little sister, who also happened to be her best friend. "Never mind, forget it. In the future, ask."

She pulled her head back and made a face that reminded me of her tantrums when she was little.

"Wow, you really aren't any fun these days, are you?" Lia looked from me over to Jones. "Don't get old—you turn into that." She pointed a finger in my direction and gave me the stink eye.

"Don't worry; Jones is only twenty-four. He has a ways to go before he's old and crabby like me," I joked. "But if he keeps hanging out with you, it'll probably speed up the process."

Lia was about to rebut but stopped when Kensy came back. I started to slide out so she could get in but stopped when the

DJ called her name for her solo song. She smiled and lifted her eyebrows excitedly before rushing to the stage again.

I leaned back in the booth and listened to her sing her heart out to a Kelly Clarkson song, and for that moment, nothing else in the world mattered. I wasn't supposed to be falling for my sister's best friend, but there was nothing to stop me at this point.

Eight
Kensy

"You said it comes furnished?" I asked, moving around the small space that might be my new home. I'd spent most of my day off hopping from place to place, trying to find something I could afford that didn't scare the bejesus out of me. For Beaumont Creek being such a beautiful place, they seemed to be lacking in the housing department.

There were a few places that I'd looked at that were gorgeous and had plenty of room, but unfortunately, I couldn't afford them. That left me with the last few apartments I was looking at and a rental house that threatened to fall apart if I closed the door too hard.

"Yes, all of the furniture you see comes with it," Cheryl, the realtor, said, pointing her index finger at the array of mismatched pieces in front of us.

I tried to hide my grimace as I eyed the blue plaid couch with cigarette burn marks in the fabric and an unmistakable stain mark on the cushion. I shuddered, hoping that I could find something better than this. *Anything better than this.*

We walked through the rest of the apartment, checking out the guest bedroom and master suite—if you could even call it that. My spirits were plummeting as I tried to plaster on a smile and promised to reach out and let her know soon if I wanted to move forward with submitting an application.

By the time I was done, I headed back to Lia's apartment and plopped down on the couch, feeling downright depressed. A few minutes later, she came in, gave me one look, then reached into the fridge and grabbed the bottle of wine we opened last night before joining me.

"That bad, huh?" she asked, pulling the cork out and taking a sip before passing the bottle to me.

I looked at her like she was crazy, but then took the bottle anyway and lifted it to my lips. The cold, sweet liquid was the best part of my day so far, which was saying a lot.

"One apartment had a resident rat named George."

"Eew." She shivered and took the bottle as I handed it to her.

"I'm sorry. I'm trying to find something so I won't be in your hair much longer."

Lia's face fell before she lifted the bottle and finished the rest of the wine in a few hefty gulps.

"What happened to sharing?" I joked with a laugh.

She got up, threw the bottle away, and grabbed another. I eyed her cautiously, wondering why we were drinking so heavily on a Wednesday night.

"What's going on?" I asked as she twisted the cap to open it. Sometimes we had expensive wine with a cork; others, we had cheap bottles with easy access when needed. Apparently, we were in need tonight, though I didn't know why.

"I, um…." She stalled for a moment, taking another drink before wiping her mouth with the back of her hand and passing the bottle to me. "I got notice today that they're increasing the rent here. Unfortunately, with books and tuition, I can't afford the increase."

"Okay," I said slowly. "What does that mean? Are you looking for a new place too?"

I took a drink while I waited for her to talk.

"I've thought about it, but honestly, I don't think there's going to be much that I can afford without ending up in a shit ho—"

She stopped talking when she realized what she was about to say.

"Without ending up in a shit hole," I finished for her. "Like me."

"I didn't mean it that way."

"I know. But honestly, that's all that's out there that I can afford. When is the increase happening?"

"Next month," she sighed.

"Holy shit. How can they do that? That's not enough time to get things situated," I exclaimed, now understanding why she decided we needed the extra wine tonight.

"Apparently, they sent notices out a few months ago, but I haven't bothered to check my mailbox, so I just now saw it."

"Lia," I muttered, holding my head in my hands. "You have to check your mail more often."

"I know, I know. It's just that 99% of my bills come through electronically, so there's no point in checking my mailbox. Other than junk mail, I don't ever get anything important."

"Until now."

"Until now," she repeated, taking another swig from the bottle.

"What are you going to do?"

"I don't know. I guess move back with my parents for a bit until I can figure something else out. There really aren't many choices. My friend Bella's lease is up in a few months, so we talked about finding a place together. Maybe we can get a 3-bedroom place, and you can move in with us?"

I'd hung out with Bella and Lia a handful of times since I'd been back and really liked her. She was super fun, sweet, and would make a great roommate. The only problem was that I had nowhere to go in the meantime.

"That sounds great and all, but I think I need to find my own place. Thanks for thinking of me, though." I swallowed another drink of wine, hoping to keep the emotion out of my voice.

"I can see if my parents can make room for you, too," Lia offered, already knowing where my head was going. "It'll be tight, but we've made this work."

"No, really," I interrupted, holding my hand up to stop her. "I'm fine, but thank you. It'll be good to get on my feet. Start over."

"Kensy," she said softly.

"I'm fine. Really." I handed the bottle back to her and got up. "I have a few things that I need to do before those family photoshoots this weekend, so I'm going to head out. I'll be back in a few hours."

She smiled but didn't try to stop me. That was the thing
with being best friends for so long; we didn't have to
tell each other when we needed a moment. I grabbed my
cell phone and keys from the counter and closed the door
behind me.

48

Nine
Capshaw

It had been three weeks since Kensy started working for us and five since my dad had been out on leave for his knee surgery. His physical therapy was going well, but he'd caught pneumonia a few weeks in and spent the past few recovering from it. The doctors finally cleared him to return to work but on light duty.

I wasn't sure what that meant for me and whether I would need to put in as many hours as I had been. With him returning, all of the monthly reports and HR stuff would go back to him, and I would only really be helping out in the kitchen or working the register if needed. I knew that Kensy had been great at catching us up, which made it hard to justify my staying on any longer.

Before, I would have been itching to go back to the firehouse and be with my platoon again, but now that Kensy was in the picture, it was difficult to want to be away from her. Not that I was *with her*, but somehow I'd still gotten rather comfortable with being in the same vicinity as her.

I sat at the desk in my dad's office at Surf 'N Shack and went over the reports for the month, knowing that I needed to get everything updated in the spreadsheet before he came back so I could make the transition easier for him. Once I was done, I shut everything down and headed to the front, where I knew Kensy would be finishing up her shift. It was Friday, which was always a half day for her since she worked longer hours Monday through Thursday and had weekends off.

It was quiet up front, with no customers and the music softly playing over the speakers. Kensy was sitting at one of the tables by the register with a stack of papers in front of her. I walked over and stood beside her, feeling the corners of my lips turn up as I spotted a handful of Sour Patch Kid candies sitting on a napkin, all of their heads bitten off.

"Do I want to know what happened to those?" I asked, more so to announce that I was standing there since she hadn't bothered to look up yet. I folded my arms over my chest and raised an eyebrow when she turned and smiled at me over her shoulder.

"Nothing happened," she laughed. "I just like to eat them head first."

"And leave the bodies behind?"

"I get to them eventually." She shrugged, picking one up and biting its head off. "Want one?"

"That depends. Do I get the full kid, or am I just eating their asses?"

The words were out of my mouth before I could stop them. I felt the heat wash over me as my cheeks flamed with embarrassment.

Kensy's eyes widened, but her grin spread quickly as she pulled her bottom lip between her teeth and turned to face me.

"I don't know. Do you like eating ass?"

I swallowed hard, forcing back all of the things I wanted to say. Instead, I cleared my throat and licked my lips.

"If you have a full kid, I'll take one." There—that was a safe answer.

She laughed as she picked up the bag and extended it to me.

I pulled one out and popped it into my mouth, noticing the way her eyes locked on and watched every movement. Even though I shouldn't have, I licked my lips again, making sure she saw how my tongue glided across it the same way it would if I were between her thighs, eating her instead.

"Thank you," I said, pulling her attention away from my mouth. "That was delicious."

"You're welcome."

I pulled the chair across from her out and sat down.

"What are you working on?"

She looked through the piles of papers in front of her beside the different colored highlighters and sighed.

"I'm looking for an apartment, and these are my options. I have to decide by tonight—technically, I was supposed to have an answer by yesterday, but I can't bring myself to pick one."

"Why not?" I asked, raising my eyebrows to ask for permission before taking one of the papers from the stack. She nodded and leaned back in her chair, allowing me some time to look over them.

"I hate them all," she chuckled. "I can't picture myself living in any of these, and the ones that I would actually consider are too expensive. So, I'm stuck and dragging my feet because I really don't want to decide. But, unless I want to be homeless, I don't have much of a choice."

I pulled my mouth to the side and flipped through the pages, studying her options. She was right—these all sucked. Not a single one was a place I would want her to live at, though it wasn't my place to say so.

"What happened with staying with Lia?" I asked, continuing to go through the pile.

"She's moving back with your parents for a while because they raised her rent, and she can't afford it anymore. Didn't she tell you?"

I looked up at her and shook my head.

"I haven't talked to Lia recently, and my mom hasn't said anything. Though I'm sure that's because she's been busy trying to get my dad situated to return to work and making sure they have everything he might need here."

"Oh, sorry for sharing the news then."

"Don't be. I appreciate you telling me. Lia's still my little sister, and I want to know when things like this happen. I'm glad she has someplace to go, but to be honest, I don't feel comfortable with you living at any of these places."

"I don't have a choice," she said sadly with a shrug. "I can't afford anything else right now without having to take a second or third job. Even with getting the photography stuff set up, I still wouldn't make enough to cover the rent *and* be able to buy groceries every month."

I slid the papers back to her and worked my jaw back and forth. I hated this for her—more so because I felt helpless and couldn't stand the thought of her living somewhere that wasn't safe or clean.

The bell above the door chimed as customers walked in.

"I'd better get back up front," she said, standing up and heading to the front. "Don't eat all of my Sour Patch Kids." She winked playfully, but all I could think about was her eating their asses, and that was a thought that had me feeling even more uneasy than I had to begin with.

54

<u>Ten</u>
Kensy

My new apartment wasn't bad, but it wasn't what you'd call good either. It was hard to believe, but it was actually smaller than Lia's apartment. It came furnished—if you could really call it that. There was a couch that had seen better days with a pullout bed included and a rickety table with pieces of cardboard taped to the bottom of the legs to try to balance it out so it wouldn't tip over.

I'd spent the weekend scrubbing everything down with bleach before I "officially" moved in—not that I had much to move to begin with. By Sunday, I had a clean fridge stocked with plenty of food and a brand-new pan to cook with. There were also a handful of cheap bottles of wine that I had splurged on to celebrate being on my own.

Growing up, my mother was never around. She was a singer and said she felt her *calling* in different bars across the country. Apparently, she also found herself called to the beds of random men she'd met along the way, which was the final straw for my dad, which ended their fifteen-year marriage when he filed for divorce.

My dad was an incredible person who did everything he could to provide for me and give me the best childhood. We didn't always have much, but he made the best of what we did have. By age seven, I had stopped asking about my mom. I was eleven when he sat me down and told me that they were getting a divorce. I guess he thought I would be more upset about it, but given that I didn't know my mom that well, I wasn't bothered by it. I simply said *okay*, then went back to reading my book.

When my dad died, I was devastated. He'd been sick for a while, so we knew that it was coming, but that didn't do anything to ease the pain when he finally passed. Even though I was thankful that he wasn't in pain or suffering anymore, there was nothing that could fix the ache in my heart that I had felt every single day since then.

Lia had come down for my dad's service, which was small, with family and friends—something we didn't have a lot of. I had tracked down my mother and asked her to come, but I wasn't surprised when she blew me off and said she couldn't make it because she was on tour. I wasn't sure which was more laughable—that I thought she would actually be a decent human being and show up or that she considered herself to be some mega superstar when no one even heard of her band.

I'd cried for hours while I packed up my dad's stuff and donated most of it to a local shelter. Lia sat with me and held me when I needed it, reminding me that everything would be okay. I kept the things that were important and said goodbye to the rest. One thing that my dad always taught me was to live humbly and not focus on the materialistic parts of life. After everything was done, I fell apart again, not knowing where I would go or what I would do. That was when Lia stepped in and asked me to move back to Beaumont Creek and live with her until I could get on my feet.

The oven timer dinged, startling me out of my thoughts. I'd planned to make a healthy dinner tonight but was too exhausted from cleaning all weekend, so I decided to settle on a frozen pizza and a premade garden salad I'd picked up at the store.

I grabbed my food, poured a glass of wine, and sat down on the couch to enjoy my first home-cooked meal in my new place. Was I all on my own and had no idea what I was doing? Absolutely. Did it terrify the shit out of me? You bet your ass. But was it going to stop me from living my life and trying to make my dad proud, even though he wasn't here to see it? Not by any means.

58

Eleven
Capshaw

"Are you sure you're ready? I don't have to go back yet. I can take more time if you need it." I sat across from my dad while he got situated behind the desk and found a way to elevate his leg.

"I'm sure," he laughed before wincing and squeezing his eyes shut as he lifted his leg higher.

My brows pulled together in worry as he waved me off and dismissed it.

"I appreciate all that you've done for me—for us, but it's plenty, Jack. I know how much being a firefighter means to you. That's your dream, and this is mine. I might be slow-moving for a bit, but we've got plenty of help with Kensy. Your mom said she's been nothing but a godsend and that she does laps around every other server we've ever hired."

"She's good," I admitted, though I had to bite my tongue to avoid letting the rest of my thoughts tumble out.

"So then, see, there's nothing to worry about." He folded his hands in front of him on the desk and smiled, the corners of his eyes wrinkling. "Now, when do you report back to the firehouse?"

"Thursday," I said with a sigh, shoving my hand back through my hair.

"Is your platoon excited to have you back?"

"I don't know. Hopefully." I laughed and shrugged. I hadn't talked to anyone but Nate to make the arrangements. Things had been busy with helping Lia move in with my parents and assisting my dad with his return to work.

"I'm sure they are," he assured me. "And I'm sure you'll enjoy getting back into your old routine."

I nodded but didn't say anything because I didn't know whether I was or not. While I missed being at the firehouse and bullshitting with the guys, it had also been nice working with Kensy and getting to know her.

We talked for a bit before I left him to have some time to himself without me hovering. I knew Kensy was already there—not because her shift was starting soon, but because I could feel it in my bones. It was like my body had a magnet in it that was instantly drawn to hers, pulled out of my control.

I rounded the corner and found her at the register, taking an order as the new busboy randomly walked through the restaurant, seeming unsure of what to do. I went over and gave him a quick reminder of what we needed from him, finishing up at the same time Kensy did.

"Hey," she said as I approached and stood beside her.

"Hey."

"How's your dad doing?"

"He seems good. Determined," I laughed. "There's no stopping him now, so it's just a matter of making sure he has everything he needs and that he's as comfortable as possible."

"Just let me know how I can help."

"I appreciate that, thank you."

Another customer walked in, interrupting me from continuing the conversation with her. I shouldn't have been surprised when more people came in right after that, given that it was the time that our rush typically started.

I sighed and walked off, heading to the kitchen to help them get started on the orders that were coming through.

By the time my shift ended, my dad had already gotten through all the paperwork he needed and was stubbornly moving around with his cane, checking on everything. I knew how much it meant for him to be back, but I also hated how I suddenly felt like I no longer had a place here.

I said goodnight to my parents and then headed out the door at the same time as Kensy.

"You headed home?" I asked, still hating the apartment she'd decided to rent. It was right on the outskirts of Beaumont Creek and was a single room above a sketchy 24-hour gas station with its fair share of shady people.

"Yeah, I'm tired. You?"

"Probably. I thought about getting a bite to eat first. Wanna join me?"

She looked down at her watch and then at the sky, noticing that the sun was already setting.

"Thanks, but I better get home. Maybe another time?"

"Okay." The words burned in my throat because it wasn't okay. It wasn't even a little bit okay that she had to hurry home before it got too late because she knew the longer she waited, the less safe it would be.

"Do you want me to follow you home?" I asked, not thinking it through before the words were out of my mouth.

Her brow furrowed as she tilted her head to look at me.

"Sorry," I corrected myself. "I just meant since it's getting dark out. I don't mind following you over to make sure you get in safe."

She smiled, but it didn't reach her eyes.

"I'm okay, but thank you. That's very sweet of you to offer."

She turned and headed for the bus station, another thing that I hated but had no right to.

I rubbed a hand along my neck, trying to ease some of the tension. It irritated me that she wouldn't accept my help, but even more so that I was so obsessed with caring for someone who didn't want it. Kensy had gotten so far under my skin that I couldn't even think straight these days. I climbed into my truck and watched her walk, knowing I would still find a way to sneak over to her apartment just to ensure she got home safe.

Twelve
Kensy

It didn't go unnoticed that Jack had followed me home again the other night, so I couldn't say that it wasn't disappointing not to have my usual secret escort tonight. But he'd started back at the firehouse today, which meant that we wouldn't be working together anymore and likely wouldn't see each other often either.

When I'd gotten off the bus tonight, I felt this strange feeling deep inside that only got worse the closer I got to my apartment. I adjusted the strap of my purse to hang across my body and then clutched my keys between my fingers, the way my dad had taught me as soon as I was old enough to be left home by myself and walk to and from school alone.

My heart raced as I looked around, trying to identify the source of my unease. As soon as I reached the door to my apartment, I knew what had happened.

The wood was split down the middle from where someone had kicked the door in. I pushed it open slowly, holding my breath as I looked around to see if anyone was still inside. At first look, it appeared that whoever it was had already left. I walked over and checked the bathroom, relieved that no one was waiting for me behind the shower curtain like in those cheesy horror movies.

I sat on the toilet lid and let out a shaky breath as my fingers trembled. I knew I couldn't stay here tonight with the door kicked in, but I didn't have anywhere else to go. There was a tiny bit of cash that I had hidden and taped to the back of the toilet tank that might be able to get me a hotel room for a few nights, but that would be pushing it.

Knowing that I needed to move quickly before it got too late, I reached down and felt around for it, my heart sinking when I grabbed the tape and pulled it loose. The money from the envelope was gone, along with my spirits.

Tears ran down my face as I tried to wipe them away. Now wasn't the time to fall apart. I needed to get my stuff and get the hell out of here. Who knew if whoever had broken in would be back again, but either way, I didn't want to be here if so.

I grabbed the duffle bag I'd brought from Texas and packed everything I had, kissing the framed photo of my dad and me before wrapping it in a scarf and tucking it inside. I gave one last look at my first *home* and then walked out before I succumbed to the disappointment that was building inside from failing already.

The gas station was busy with guys hanging out, looking for their next score as I walked past them. There were a handful of catcalls, along with one of them trying to grab my arm before I slipped out of his grip and kept going. The bus would be coming again in five minutes; I just had to push myself to get there in time. I was tired, and my body hurt from working all day, but if I missed the bus, I would be stuck there, and this wasn't a place I wanted to be.

A few minutes later, I was panting as I ran the last few steps to the bus stop, reaching it just as the bus was getting ready to pull away. I climbed on, paid my fare, and took a seat in the back, slumping down onto the seat as the weight of my day collapsed on me.

I pulled my phone out, hoping it would give me a sign as to what I should do, but instead, I just sat there, staring at it. I could call Lia, but I knew there wasn't much she could do. She was back at her parent's house, but it was beyond cramped, with no extra space for me to invade. I started looking up hotels as we approached the first few stops on Main Street.

Surf 'N Shack was the next stop, and before I could stop myself, I was getting off the bus and heading inside. There weren't many places that I had found around town where I felt truly safe and comfortable, but this was it.

I went inside and sat down at one of the booths in the back, taking a moment to gather myself and catch my breath. It was busy with the evening crowd coming through, so I knew that I could hang out for a bit without drawing attention to myself. I debated going up and grabbing something for dinner, but I needed to save up every penny I had right now until I could figure out my next step.

I took a few minutes and called my landlord to report the break-in. He wasn't surprised and agreed to let me out of my lease early if I didn't get the cops involved. While I didn't love how shady he was being about it, I also didn't see the point in bringing the police into it. Aside from the cash taped to the toilet, they didn't steal anything else from me, and I knew I would never see the money. Honestly, it was less headache if I just let it go and move on. I did, however, get the sleazy landlord to agree to refund the full month's rent plus the deposit, given I hadn't even lived there an entire month and was keeping him off of law enforcement's radar.

My head was down as I chewed my nail nervously while scrolling through nearby lodging options. There were a few hotels with rooms available, but because they were on Main Street, they were more than I could afford. I looked into some of the classified ads, hoping that maybe another single woman my age was looking for a sane roommate, but I came up empty-handed.

I felt the tension build in my neck as a headache started wrapping around the front of my head. I reached into my purse and looked around for a granola bar, frustrated when I came up empty.

"Hey, what are you doing here?"

I looked up to find Jack standing in front of me, wearing his firefighter gear and looking sexier than he had any right to look.

"Hey," I replied, my words getting caught in my throat. I seriously couldn't think about anything other than how hot he looked right now.

"Everything okay?" he asked, turning the chair around before straddling it.

Fuck. Me.

Literally—fuck me. Right here. Right now. Leave the gear on and put out this fucking fire burning inside me.

"Yeah," I stuttered, looking anywhere but at his face. I knew that once I did, he would immediately know something was wrong, and I couldn't handle that right now.

"Kensy."

My name was a warning on his lips.

My eyes lifted and met his. The features flashed across his face as he studied me.

"What happened?" he asked, his voice gruff.

"Nothing," I lied, looking down again.

"Kensy. I'm not playing—what happened?"

"Nothing. I just thought I'd hang out here tonight."

"Bullshit. You don't ever just *hang out* here after your shifts. You go home, but since you're not there, that tells me that something happened, and I want to know what it is. Now."

I let my shoulders fall with the breath I exhaled heavily.

"My apartment got broken into."

"What?" His eyebrows rose high on his forehead, nearly escaping into his tousled hair. "Did you call the cops?"

I shook my head and looked out the window to avoid meeting his eyes again.

"There's nothing they would have done. I spoke to the landlord, and he agreed to give me back the deposit and full month's rent if I didn't report it."

He muttered something under his breath, but I couldn't hear it.

"Are you okay?" His tone softened as he continued to study me.

"Yeah, I'm fine. I wasn't there when it happened. They kicked in the door and stole the cash I had taped to the back of the toilet."

"Fuck," he muttered, shaking his head. "So you came back here?"

I shrugged, still refusing to look at him.

"I felt safe here and didn't have anywhere else to go. I've been looking for hotels, but since they took what cash I did have, there isn't much that I can afford with what I have in my checking account. I put almost everything I had into securing the lease on that apartment."

My heart raced in my chest as I tried to force the tears back once again. The last thing I wanted was for Jack to see me falling apart. I pulled my shoulders back and took in a deep breath.

"You're not staying in a hotel," he said sternly.

"I know," I said with a bit of a crazy laugh, the emotions bubbling up inside of me. "I can't afford one. I think we've already covered that I am officially homeless with no place to go. My dad would be so proud of me."

The last few words got caught in my throat as I blinked back the tears that were already started to fall. I covered my face with my hands and tried to hide the sob that escaped. I heard Jack's chair scrape across the floor before he got up and wrapped his arms around me.

"It's going to be okay, Kensy," he assured me as he held me tighter.

"How?" I asked, pulling away and wiping the tears away with my fingers. "I literally have nowhere to go, Jack. I've hit rock bottom with no way back up."

He looked up and nodded to the guys waiting for him at the front of the restaurant with their to-go bags, then reached into his pocket, pulling out a set of keys.

"I'll get you a copy made, but for now, you can take mine

and get yourself situated. There's a guest bedroom with a bed and a dresser that you can use. It's right across from the bathroom that will be yours. I'm on a 48-hour shift, so I won't be home until Saturday morning. We can sit down and figure out the other details then. For now, help yourself to food and whatever else you need." He handed me the keys and nodded for me to take them.

"Jack, I can't."

"You don't have a choice, Kensy. I didn't want you living in that apartment, to begin with, but I sure as hell am not allowing you to live on the streets. Take the keys and go to my house. I'll have the guys drop you off on our way back to the firehouse."

My jaw stayed hanging open in disbelief. No one had ever done something this nice for me, and I couldn't believe that Jack was really suggesting that I live with him.

"I need to talk to the guys real quick, but get your stuff so we can go."

He gave me a pointed look and then walked back to the front, yelling something at Frankie before stopping to talk to his platoon. I picked up the duffle bag and hung it on my shoulder, ready to take the next step.

Thirteen
Capshaw

"You really didn't need to do all of this," Kensy said, motioning to the bag filled with food from Surf 'N Shack that was sitting on her lap while we rode to my house. I'd given Nate a heads up about the extra stop, and somehow, we were able to squeeze Kensy in the back of the truck between us, putting her almost sitting on my lap—which I didn't mind in the least.

"You need to eat, and I didn't trust that you would help yourself to the food at my house," I replied, looking out the window as I struggled with keeping my hands from reaching out to brush the strand of hair out of her face.

"Well, thank you. I can have them take it from my check when I go in tomorrow."

"That's not necessary. Just enjoy the food."

"How did you know what I liked?" she asked, her voice loud enough for me to hear but quiet enough to be drowned out by the other guys talking.

Because I know everything about you, Kensy.

"I've seen you order it a few times."

"Oh, duh." She pressed the palm of her hand to her head and laughed. "Sorry, I'm tired and not thinking straight right now."

"You've had a long day," I agreed as we pulled up in front of my house. I waited for Rodriguez to put the truck in park, then climbed down and helped Kensy out.

We went to the door, and I waited for her to unlock it, making sure she didn't have any trouble with the lock since it would sometimes stick. Thankfully, it didn't give her any fits and opened right away.

She walked inside while I turned on the lights behind her. I gave her a quick tour of the house, making sure to point out where the guestroom was. Not that I didn't want her in my bedroom—I just couldn't handle the thought of it right now when I was stuck on shift with the guys for another thirty-some hours. I took her through the kitchen, showed her where to find everything, and made her promise that she would help herself to anything she wanted in the fridge and pantry.

Once she was settled in, I walked out and felt the nagging tingling sensation from knowing she was in my house. It was going to be hard going back to work and being able to focus after this.

****

The rest of my shift was uneventful, aside from the guys giving me shit about having Kensy stay with me. I tried to argue that I wouldn't be affected by it, but we all knew it was a lie. While they were convinced that I would lose my mind and go crazy living with a girl, I was more worried that I would give into the temptation that I had been fighting for so long now.

Saturday morning, I stopped and grabbed breakfast and coffee, knowing that Kensy was already up. She had texted me to ask when I would be home since she had the only copy of the keys to my house at the moment.

I was equally nervous and excited about seeing her, which made me feel even more awkward by the time I got there. She was standing at the door, a smile plastered across her face as she waited for me to get out of the truck. It was weird that my immediate thought was a flash forward to coming home to this one day, with her as my wife. I shook my head, trying to clear the thought, all while pretending not to be bothered by her being there.

"Good morning," she said cheerfully, closing the door behind me as I set the coffee and food down on the island.

"Morning," I replied, offering her a smile so she didn't think I didn't want her there. The truth was, I was tired from not sleeping ever since I knew she was going to be living with me. "You're up early."

I pulled the food out of the bag and set it on the counter, hoping I got her order right. I didn't have any idea what she liked, so I'd sunk as low as texting Lia to ask since they had lived together for a while, and she should know since she was her best friend.

"I'm always up early. My dad used to say that there was no use in wasting the day away when you could get up early and take the bull by the horns."

"Good motto."

"Yeah, it's always stuck with me. I like to get up early and get things done so I can enjoy the rest of the day without worrying about things on my to-do list. Which speaking of, I hope you don't mind that I ran the load of laundry that was in the hamper. I also folded the clothes that were in the dryer and set them on your bed. I'm sorry, I should have asked before going into your room—"

"You did my laundry?" I asked, stopping what I was doing so I could look at her.

She swallowed hard as a pinkish hue tinted her cheeks.

"I'm sorry. I shouldn't have assumed—"

"Kensy, I'm not mad that you did my laundry," I sighed heavily, shoving my hand through my hair. "I just wasn't expecting it. But you're my roommate, not my maid. Please don't worry about cleaning up after me. I'll make sure to keep the laundry room more tidy so you can use it when needed without having to worry about my stuff."

"I honestly didn't mind," she said with a laugh. "Laundry is soothing to me."

I raised an eyebrow as I stacked her hashbrown on the plate next to the sausage and egg biscuit sandwich.

"You find laundry to be soothing?" I questioned as I finished platting my food and handed hers to her.

"Thank you for this," she said as she took the plate and sat down at the kitchen table. "And yes, I find it very soothing."

"Not me," I joked, sitting opposite her. "That's probably why I let it sit so long. I go through all of my clean clothes just to avoid having to do it."

She laughed and covered her mouth with a napkin as she chewed.

"That explains why there was so much for just one person," she teased. "I also did the load of towels and got those put away."

"Thank you. You really didn't have to do all of that."

"I don't mind. It's the least I can do for you letting me stay here. And I promise—I'll be out of your hair as soon as possible."

"It's not a problem; you don't have to rush to find a new place. Honestly, I feel better about you staying with me than I do with you going back to something like you had before. I know finding a decent place to stay in Beaumont Creek is expensive, but you shouldn't settle or risk your safety."

She smiled and took a bite of her biscuit, her tongue slipping out to catch a crumb before it fell. I looked away and focused on swallowing my bites without choking on them.

Once we were finished with breakfast, I headed to my bedroom and found the stack of clothes she'd mentioned. I put them away, then jumped in the shower to cool off. Usually, I would come home and sleep for a few hours, which was what I really wanted to do, but having Kensy there made me anxious to get back out there and spend time with her. I was in deep and sinking by the second.

Fourteen
Kensy

A flash of lightning startled me as I walked into the kitchen to get a drink of water. I'd had a restless night as it was, knowing that Jack was asleep just a few doors down the hall from me. On top of the stupid aching I felt between my thighs every time he got too close, the thunder from an unexpected storm had jolted me awake and interrupted the highly inappropriate dream that had me on edge with the cruelest tease of release just at my fingertips.

I fumbled along the wall, looking for the light switch before I woke Jack up by breaking something in the middle of the night. I had only been here a few days, so it wasn't like I had everything memorized yet with where everything was. The thunder rolled outside as the storm raged on, the sky beautifully illuminated by the flashes of light dancing across it.

Just as my fingers found the switch to turn the lights on, I heard a loud noise outside and jumped. My heart raced inside my chest, making me regret getting up to get a drink of water. I wasn't usually scared of much, but bad weather always got to me. I flipped the switch a few times, frustrated when the lights didn't turn on.

"The power is out," Jack said from what sounded like the other side of the room. It was pitch black, so I couldn't tell where he was and had to rely on the sound of his voice to try to locate him. Hell, at this point, I wasn't even sure where *I* was in the kitchen, everything was off, and I had already lost my sense of direction.

"Holy fuck," I blurted out, holding a hand to my chest as I tried to calm myself from being startled. "You scared the shit out of me."

"Sorry, I came for a glass of water. Didn't know you were in here until I heard you flipping the switch. Which, by the way, that one is for the garbage disposal."

"Shit," I muttered, reaching over again to make sure I put it back in the off position. That could be a terrible wake-up call neither of us needed if the power came back on in the middle of the night while we were sleeping. "Sorry, I don't know where things are and was coming for a glass of water myself."

"Don't be sorry. I told you to make yourself at home. You're allowed to get up and get stuff in the middle of the night, Kensy."

I looked away, embarrassed, though he couldn't see me. Why did I feel like such a kid around him? Maybe it was the tone he used when he said my name, making sure I knew that he only thought of me as Lia's best friend and nothing else.

"Thank you," I said quietly, unsure of what else to say.

I heard him moving around the kitchen, opening drawers on the island and closing them, though I wasn't sure what he was looking for.

"There should be flashlights in one of the drawers on your side," he said, the sound of his footsteps filling the air as he approached.

I blindly reached down and patted the area around me with my hands, trying to find the handle for the drawers he was talking about. I opened one and started feeling around for anything that might feel like a flashlight. I couldn't tell what was in it, but it felt a bit like being Goldilocks, with things being too big and too small to be what I was looking for.

Goosebumps erupted over my skin as Jack stood next to me. I felt his fingers graze lightly over mine as we reached to open the next drawer at the same time. Instinctively, I pulled my hand away and waited for him to open it. I moved to the side, hoping that I was out of the way.

The smell of his body wash wafted in the air around me, making me feel dizzy. Maybe it was the blackout and not having any idea what my surroundings were, but I chose to blame his intoxicating scent instead.

"Any luck?" he asked, his voice velvety smooth and snapping me out of my thoughts.

"Oh, sorry. I wasn't looking." I laughed nervously and turned to help.

I hated not being able to see anything as I reached forward, opening and closing my fingers as they gripped something thick, round, and hard.

"I think I found it," I said excitedly, gripping it harder while Jack let out an awkward-sounding groan. "Here it is!"

I pulled hard, frowning when I was met with resistance until his body was suddenly right in front of mine.

"That's not a flashlight." His words sounded strained as they came out of his mouth.

"I'm pretty sure it is," I argued, pulling it harder again. "It's in some sort of fabric case, but I know what a flashlight feels like, Jack." I rolled my eyes at how much he doubted me right now.

"No, Kensy," he gritted out. "That's my cock."

"But it's hard. And round. And firm," I objected, still failing to let go of it.

"That's because you won't stop pulling on it, and it's making it hard."

My mouth fell open as I realized the truth in his words. My fingers grazed against the soft fabric of his boxer briefs before I pulled away, freeing him from my grip.

"Oh my GOD!" I screamed, covering my eyes as if I could possibly see anything to begin with. "JACK! Why was it hard to begin with?"

I was mortified as the words kept tumbling out of my mouth, no matter how hard I tried to stop them. I heard him chuckle and step away. Thank God, I couldn't think straight when he was this close to me—obviously.

"I was having some, um *dreams*, then decided to get up to get a drink of water to try to cool off. Then you started grabbing and yanking on it, making it *harder*."

"I'm so sorry," I apologized as quickly as I could. "I didn't know. I thought it was a flashlight. It felt like it. I mean, I just thought maybe you had a super fancy one that had its own carrying case. I mean, if I knew that it was your dic— *penis*, I would never have touched it, let alone pulled on it as hard as I did. Did I break it? Is it possible to dislocate a coc—*penis*? Oh my God, should I go online and look on WebMD to see if we need to do anything? What if it's sprained? Can we get a splint or something? Should I call Li—"

"For the love of God, I'm begging you not to finish that sentence," he warned, his hand somehow finding me in the darkness and resting on my shoulder to stop me. "Please don't *ever* mention my sister or my cock in the same sentence."

I bit my tongue to keep from saying anything else.

"Okay," I agreed. "But is there something we need to do for *it*?"

"For my cock?"

"Yes," I whispered, butterflies swarming through my stomach every time he said the word *cock*. "I know that we don't have power right now, but I can grab my phone and see if it has enough battery to use the flashlight if you want to look at it."

"I think I'm good, but thank you," he chuckled.

"I feel so terrible. I can't believe I did that."

He stepped away and let his hand fall from my shoulder.

"Don't worry about it. It's fine."

"It's not," I laughed. "It's so embarrassing!"

"Well, I guess I should be flattered," he teased. "I've had a lot of compliments before, but I don't think I've ever heard of anyone mistaking it for a flashlight. I mean, I guess it could light up the darkest of nights—if used right."

My jaw hung open as I listened to his words. It felt like he was flirting with me, but given that I couldn't see him to read his face right now, I didn't want to make any more mistakes and further embarrass myself.

"I should probably get back to bed," I offered, twisting my hands together in front of me. "Sorry about the um—you know."

"Yeah, not a problem. Did you want a drink first?"

I pulled my head back in surprise and replayed his question in his head.

"A drink? Like alcohol or do you mean from your…."

"Of water, Kensy. Did you still want a drink of water?"

I could hear the humor in his voice.

"Oh. Yeah. Um, no, I think I'm okay. I'm just going to go lay down and hope that the darkness of the universe sucks me up so I can forget that this night ever happened."

"Okay," he laughed. "But if you need something to light up the night, you know where to find me."

I heard his footsteps as they walked past me before the sink turned on, and he filled a glass of water. I turned and felt along the walls, praying that I made it back to my bed without any other problems tonight.

Fifteen
Capshaw

Kensy avoided me for days, and I couldn't say I didn't blame her. I knew she was embarrassed about what happened Saturday night, though I purposely avoided mentioning it. By Tuesday, I was back on another 48-hour shift, and it seemed it was the break both of us needed.

After she mistook my cock for a flashlight, I couldn't get the dirty thoughts of her out of my head. From the second I felt her fingers wrap around me, I knew that it would forever be engrained in my spank bank. It wasn't even that she'd touched me—it was that she hadn't stopped. Like she was genuinely convinced that it was something *other* than a dick in her hand as she tugged and gripped it tightly.

My dream that night had been vivid and included Kensy on her knees, taking me down her throat as my hand wound tightly in her hair. I tried to shake it off but couldn't. Instead of giving in and jacking off to my little sister's best friend, I had decided that a cold glass of water was a better option. At least I wouldn't be flooded with guilt about it later.

But that all changed the second my mind registered what was happening and my dream came flooding back, making me rock fucking hard for her. After she went to bed—which I made sure she made it to the right one before I went to mine—I laid down and processed what the fuck had just happened. It hadn't even been a full 24 hours of being alone with Kensy in my house, and we'd already crossed the line I had been working so hard not to. But in all fairness, it wasn't on purpose, and weirder things had happened.

"What's up with you this morning?" Nate asked as he sat at the table and lifted his breakfast sandwich to his mouth.

"Nothing," I lied, taking a drink of coffee before finishing off the rest of my food so I could get up and find something productive to do, AKA keep my mind off thoughts of Kensy.

"Bullshit," Rodriguez added from the sink. "He's been super weird this morning."

"Having a hard time with Kensy staying with you?" Nate asked, meeting my eyes as I tried to avoid looking at him.

"Something like that," I muttered, not wanting to admit just how *hard* it had been.

"Give it some time; you guys will adjust to each other in no time." Nate crumpled the paper wrapper and tossed it into the trash while I tried not to think about how I would love for us to *adjust to each other*. My mind was a complete wasteland these days, ridden with dirty thoughts that I had no place to have about my little sister's best friend.

I'd been beating myself up about it—figuratively, not literally—since Saturday night when I made the mistake of giving in and letting myself flirt with Kensy. I knew better, but it was like there was some sort of forcefield surrounding us that allowed me to act in the moment and say the things I really wanted to say. What was even more disturbing was that she didn't seem to be bothered by what

I said, and for a quick moment, I thought she was going to take me up on my offer to light up her night for her. Needless to say, I'd been obsessed with showing Kensy some *fireworks* ever since.

"Yeah, I'm sure we will," I said dismissively and got up.

"Hey—I meant to ask," Nate said, standing up and walking beside me. "Do you think you could talk to Kensy about doing some photos for us? I spoke to the Chief, and they wanted to do a fundraiser for the animal shelter since they need a new roof and some upgrades to the facility. He thought we could do a calendar again since that went over so well the last time we did one. Maybe Kensy can do the photos for us since she's trying to start her photography business?"

"I can ask her when I go home," I offered, shoving my hands into my pockets.

He scrunched his nose and shook his head.

"Do you think you can text her and find out? Chief needs an answer soon so he can make other arrangements if not. He's hoping to get the photos done in a few weeks and will have to find someone else if she can't."

"Okay," I sighed, chewing the inside of my cheek. "I'll ask her and see."

"Thanks." He clapped my shoulder and walked off to his office while I pulled out my phone to get this over with.

Me: Hey, would you be interested in doing a photo shoot for the firehouse?

I sat down and tapped my fingers on the table while I waited for her reply. I knew she was working at Surf 'N

Shack today, so I wasn't expecting an immediate response, even though that was exactly what I got.

Kensy: What kind of photoshoot?

Me: I'm not sure of the full details, but it will be for a calendar that we'll be selling to raise money for the Beaumont Creek Animal Shelter.

Kensy: Awww! I love dogs!! Sure, I'll do it. Do you know when?

Me: I don't, but I can find out the details and get back to you, or I can have them contact you directly if that's easier.

Kensy: It doesn't matter to me. I just need to make sure to put it on my calendar so I don't book something else.

Me: No problem. Sounds like the photography stuff is starting to take off for you.

Kensy: Here and there. I actually wanted to talk to you about something….

I swallowed hard, wondering if this was her way of finally addressing the elephant in the room we'd both been ignoring.

Me: Sure. What's up?

Kensy: I'll make it quick since my break is almost over, but I was wondering if it would be okay if I used the guest bedroom at your house for a session this weekend?

I knew that most of her sessions usually took place outdoors, somewhere by the water, where there were lots of breathtaking scenes, so I wasn't sure what she could possibly want to use my guest room for.

Me: Um, sure.

The dots bounced on the screen for a few minutes before her text finally came through.

Kensy: I don't want to make you uncomfortable using your house that way. I can find another location. It's not a problem.

Me: I'm not uncomfortable. I guess I just didn't expect you to have a family that would want their photos in there. There's nothing special about the room, so it seems like it would be a bit of a letdown, given the work I've seen you do.

Kensy: Ummm.

Kensy: It's not a family session.

My fingers hovered over the phone, not sure how to respond. I had no idea what kind of session she was talking about or why she was so nervous about it.

Kensy: It's a boudoir session.

I opened a browser and quickly typed in "boudoir photography," then closed it when a slew of photos of women wearing sexy lingerie popped up.

Kensy: Like I said, it's no big deal. I can find another place to do them.

Me: It's fine. Just tell me when and I'll make sure I'm out of the house.

Kensy: Are you sure? I don't want to make you uncomfortable.

Me: I promise.

Kensy: Okay, thank you. I've gotta get back to work,

my break is over. Thanks for thinking of me for the photos, I can't wait!

Me: No problem.

I shoved my phone across the table and scrubbed a hand over my face. Having Kensy stay with me was proving to be a bigger problem than I thought and for all of the wrong reasons.

Sixteen
Kensy

"Right there—hold that pose." I snapped a few pictures and then checked the images quickly before giving Jones a thumbs-up. "Got it, thank you!"

I lowered my camera and let it hang from the strap around my neck, waiting for them to figure out who was going next. When I first accepted this gig, I had pictured adorable puppies and firefighters in full gear. What I got was HOT firefighters without shirts on and puppies that were so stinking cute that they made the guys look even hotter.

"How's it going?" Nate asked, standing beside me and lifting a cup of coffee to his lips.

"Pretty good. I think we're about halfway through. We've done January through May, and I think June was ready, but his dog just peed on him." I pointed to where Rodriguez was standing, holding a squirmy Dalmatian as far away from his body as possible as a stream of urine sprayed in front of him.

"Guess we'll have to move on to July and come back to him," he chuckled. "I'll go see if Jackson is ready."

"Thanks."

I went back to checking the images on my camera while I waited. Thankfully, the bay doors had been opened, allowing plenty of natural light in, so I didn't have to set up much. It was also going to make editing a breeze later.

Nate had worked on getting the guys set up this morning, as well as the captain for the other platoon. It was fun watching the camaraderie between them as they busted each other's balls and talked shit about which platoon was better. I was nervous about being stuck in a room full of men, being the only girl, but they instantly made me feel at home without any awkwardness. Well, aside from the massive amount that still lingered between Jack and me after I mistook his cock for a flashlight.

Things with us had been tense, with neither of us wanting to bring it up, though I couldn't get over the idea that he had been flirting with me. I wanted to ask him about it, but how could I without risking embarrassing myself?

"Alright, Santiago is ready," Nate said, startling me.

"Oh, perfect," I replied, clearing out of the preview screen so I could start shooting again.

A very tall, muscular man with abs that looked like they went on for days stood there looking at me, waiting for guidance on what I wanted him to do, but all I could focus on was the teeny tiny teacup poodle in his giant hands.

"I know," he laughed. "They thought giving the big guy the smallest dog would be hilarious. I'm afraid to sneeze because I don't want to hurt this sweet girl."

I covered my mouth with my hand to hide my smile.

"It is quite the pairing," I agreed, noticing the Great Dane standing next to a guy who was quite a few feet shorter than Santiago. "Um, why don't we have you sit on the top step with her cuddled to your chest?" I pointed to the open door on the firetruck.

He grinned a panty-melting smile and climbed up effortlessly, moving the pup closer to his face, where she began showering him with kisses. His eyes closed as his smile spread tighter, showcasing his dimples. I started shooting, capturing the moment without knowing whether it would go on the calendar.

"That's perfect," I said, continuing to rapid click.

He pulled her away slightly and opened his eyes, holding her beside his face as if they were taking selfies. I captured the rest of the photos and thanked him as he climbed down, and the next guy got ready.

By the time we got through October, I realized I hadn't seen Jack yet. I knew he was there because I spotted him when I first arrived. It was his day off and I had left work early, so we didn't come together. I was surprised that he wasn't going to be in the calendar unless he was one of the last 3 guys. Between the two platoons, there were enough guys to fill the full 12 months, plus one for the cover and one for the back—unless I had miscounted.

I was waiting for them to finish moving the fire truck out of the bay so we could utilize the ladder when I spotted Nate struggling to carry an overweight boxer wearing a pumpkin costume. Nate was in his regular gear—shirtless like the other guys—but had a pumpkin painted on his chest to match the dog.

"If that paint rubs off, I'm going to be mad," a girl's voice warned.

I spun around to find his wife, Abby, walking beside me, shaking her head and trying not to laugh.

"I told him not to try to carry that beast," she laughed. "But noooo, he insisted it was fine and didn't weigh more than Penny."

My cheeks split as laughter erupted out of me. I'd met Abby when I did family photos for them and knew immediately that this dog weighed at least three times as much as Penny.

"Yeah, I think he might be a little off on the weight," I joked.

Nate set the dog down and exhaled heavily as he tried to catch his breath.

"Okay, where do you want me?"

I raised my eyebrows, trying to figure out a change of plans because I was planning to have him stand in the back, on the ladder, which I couldn't do now with that massive dog.

"Ummm…"

The dog flopped to the ground, let out a gargled whimper as its eyes fluttered closed, and went to sleep.

They were still standing in front of the fire truck, so I could use that as a backdrop, but I needed something more. I tapped my finger to my chin as I scanned the area, looking for anything I could use as a prop.

"What did you do to get stuck with the sleeping dog?" Peralta, the other captain, asked as he joined Abby and me while we stared at Nate.

"Perks of being a captain, I guess." He shrugged.

I tilted my head to the side, ideas rushing through it.

"You know, we don't have you in any of the photos," I said, turning my attention to Peralta.

"Yeah," he replied quietly, rocking back on his heels. "I did that on purpose."

"What if we changed that?"

"No, no, no," he objected, holding his hands up.

"What did you have in mind?" Nate asked.

"Well, since I can't use the ladder for your pictures as I had planned, I thought doing one of both captains might be fun. We could move that crate over and set it between you guys. Maybe have you arm wrestle to see who the better captain is, all while this massive guard dog sleeps on the job."

"That's not a bad idea," Nate said, eyebrows lifted as he nodded.

"I don't know." Peralta scrubbed a hand down his face.

"You afraid that I'll win?" Nate challenged.

Suddenly Peralta's face changed, and his shoulders pulled back.

"Afraid? Of you? Never."

"Prove it."

"You're on." Peralta winked at Abby and me before heading off to get changed.

A few minutes later, both guys were set up on opposite sides of the crate, with the firetruck behind him and the sleeping dog in front. I laughed as the guys joined around, talking shit about the other platoon while Nate and Peralta arm wrestled. I shot in rapid succession, making sure to capture every single second. I would go through and cull the photos later, but I knew there would be a handful of hilarious ones they would want for their own personal collection.

We wrapped up their photos, and then I moved on to Mr. November, which happened to be one of the nicest guys I'd ever met. He was the oldest firefighter in Beaumont Creek, and they paired him with one of the senior dogs, creating the most beautiful photos I had seen. Needless to say, it was the perfect option for November because he gave us all something to be thankful for, and it wasn't just him keeping his shirt on so we didn't have to see his wrinkled body, according to him.

I was looking around, debating between using the ladder for the final setting or doing something different, when I heard a deep voice behind me.

"Where do you want me?"

I spun around, my heart racing, as I locked eyes with Jack. He wasn't wearing a shirt, just like the other guys, and held a dachshund tucked under his arm as it licked his face.

"Ummm." My throat was dry as I fought the urge to tell him *exactly where I wanted him.* "I want you on the ladder."

My eyes widened as I said it, his lip twitching slightly in response.

"The ladder?"

I nodded.

"Yeah, it's big. And sturdy. Hard."

What the hell was I saying?

"You can really hold on to it. Grip it tightly."

I shook my head. Someone needed to shut me up already, but yet no one seemed to know that I was drowning in my words other than Jack, who looked quite amused by my blundering.

"Do you think you can climb to the middle and lean back on it?" I asked, praying that I could focus on anything other than his stupid pecs that were calling to me.

"Yeah, I can do that."

He walked to the truck as I followed a little too closely, forcing his body into mine when he suddenly stopped and turned around.

"Sorry," I muttered, tucking a strand of hair behind my ear while avoiding looking up at him.

"It's okay. I was going to see if you could hold my wiener dog?"

My jaw dropped open as my eyes whipped up to his.

"Excuse me?"

"The dog, Kensy. Can you hold the dog so I don't drop it?"

"Oh," I stammered. "Sure. Yeah. Okay."

I held my hands out and took it, scolding myself for hearing what I wanted to. There was no way that Jack was going to come straight out and ask me to hold his *wiener*. I rolled my eyes and smiled when the dog licked my face.

Jack hopped up onto the truck and began climbing the ladder, checking with me to see how far I wanted him to go.

"Right there is good," I said, wondering how I would get the dog to him now that he was up so high.

"I've got it," Jones said as if reading my mind. He held out his hands, took the dog, and jogged over to the truck. Within seconds he was already handing it off to Jack.

I got into position and waited for Jack to be ready before I began shooting. My fingers trembled as they pressed the button, praying that these were in focus. I hated the effect that he had on me and didn't want them to regret hiring me to do this if I messed it up because I thought he'd asked me to hold his wiener.

He smiled and cuddled the dog enough to make the pictures look good, but his eyes were focused on me the entire time. It felt like there was no one else in the room, almost like we were being given an intimate moment to connect, which sent a jolt straight through me.

Seventeen
Capshaw

I'd spent a lot of time at the gym lately to burn off the increasing frustration that seemed to constantly build whenever I was around Kensy—which was all the time now that she lived with me. Aside from when we were at work, we were always in each other's space, and I was finding it harder and harder to keep my distance from her.

After the photoshoot, we'd both come home at the same time, which meant that we couldn't avoid each other if we tried. I was going to make an excuse to go to the gym again, but I knew that people would start wondering what was wrong with me if I suddenly just lived there. I'd been there for three hours this morning before I went to the firehouse for the photos, so it wasn't like I could go back there and there was nothing else to do in Beaumont Creek on a Thursday night.

Kensy was at the kitchen table with her laptop loading the images while I opened and closed the refrigerator at least a dozen times, not remembering what was inside while I tried to figure out what to make for dinner.

"Everything okay over there?" she asked without looking up from the screen.

"Yeah, just trying to figure out dinner."

"I was going to cook something in a minute. Want me to make something for you too?"

"You don't have to cook for me, Kensy."

"I don't mind." She moved the mouse around and clicked it a few times before standing up and finally looking at me. "Does anything sound good?"

I shrugged and let out a heavy breath as I watched her move around the island in the short cotton shorts she had changed into when we got home. There was definitely something I wanted to eat…

"I'm not picky."

She pulled her mouth to the side and opened the fridge, scanning the contents inside.

"I have some leftover rotisserie chicken from last night that we could use for tacos," she offered, pulling it out of the fridge. "Plus, there are some avocados that are going to go bad soon. I can make guacamole."

"Sounds good. What can I help with?"

"Do you know how to make margaritas?" she asked, grabbing the rest of the stuff she needed from the fridge and setting it on the island.

"I do," I said with a smile, loving the way her eyes lit up.

"Great. I'll work on dinner; you work on the drinks."

She brushed past me, her touch sending chills across my skin as my fingers flexed at my sides to keep from reaching out and touching her.

We both worked on our own sides of the kitchen, my stomach growling as I smelled the chicken she was warming up and seasoning in the skillet. She dipped tortillas in another skillet filled with oil, letting them get crispy and golden before pulling them out and setting them on a paper towel to absorb the excess oil. I'd eaten tacos a million times before in my life, but nothing compared to what Kensy was making.

Finally, dinner was ready and she cleared her laptop from the table so we could eat. After salting the rim, I filled two glasses with ice and felt her eyes on me as she watched me pour the margaritas. I wasn't sure how strong they were because I had been a bit distracted by her while I was making them.

I set the pitcher on the island and then sat at the table, impressed with the spread of tacos in front of us. Kensy grinned as she reached over and grabbed a taco, lifting it to her mouth before it even got to her plate. She closed her eyes, and a soft moan escaped as she took the first bite.

"Oh my God, this is so good."

I shifted in my seat, tugging at my jeans for some relief as I imagined her saying the same thing about me as I slammed inside of her.

I reached forward and grabbed a taco, needing something to occupy my mouth so I didn't make a fool of myself by saying something stupid.

But the second the food hit my tongue and the flavors exploded, I was just as gone as she was. I had no choice but to close my eyes and allow myself to succumb to the delicious, savory taste that wanted to consume me.

"This is fucking amazing," I said, wiping the corners of my mouth as I shoved another bite in. "Thank you, Kensy."

"It's just tacos," she giggled, hiding her mouth behind a napkin.

"This is not *just tacos*," I corrected. "This is the best fucking taco I've ever had—and I've eaten a lot of tacos."

Her cheeks flushed, turning her fair skin a pretty shade of pink. I could have made an effort to correct what I had said, but I didn't bother. I knew better than to let things keep going between us, but I also couldn't stop myself around her.

"I'm glad you like my tacos."

I was mid-swallow when she said it, which forced me to choke on my bite. I covered my mouth with my fist and coughed, hoping that this wasn't how I would go out.

"Oh my goodness, are you okay?"

She got up and rushed over to my side of the table, smacking me on the back to help dislodge the food.

I held my hand up, trying to indicate that I was okay, but she kept pounding, trying to position herself behind me.

"I'm okay," I sputtered out, not sure whether I liked the beating she was giving me or not.

I mean, on the one hand, Kensy was touching me, and I loved every bit of that. But on the other—I was going to have bruises that I would have to explain to the guys, and choking on Kensy's taco didn't sound like the best thing to confess right now.

"Are you sure?" she asked, still thumping me in the back.

"Yeah," I said with a laugh, reaching back to grab her hand. "But I might not be if you don't stop clobbering me."

Her eyes widened as she realized she was still trying to hit me with her hand balled into a fist.

"I'm so sorry!"

"It's okay," I chuckled, watching as she returned and sat down. "I appreciate you trying to help."

She lifted her glass to her lips and took a long drink.

"I feel bad that my taco tried to kill you."

Do not reply to that. Just let it go. She didn't mean it the way you think she did, you pervert.

But also—what a fucking way to die.

"It didn't," I lied. "It was my fault for not chewing well before I swallowed."

We ate quietly for a few minutes, enjoying the tacos this time. Eventually, we made small talk about how things were going at work and how my dad was doing now that he was back in the swing of things. Once dinner was done, I helped clean up and felt the unease of not knowing what to do with myself for the rest of the night.

"Want a refill?" I asked, lifting the pitcher as she put the last plate into the dishwasher.

"Sure, that would be great. Thank you."

I topped our glasses off and then washed the pitcher while she set her laptop up on the table again.

"How did the photos go today?" I asked over my shoulder once I turned the water off.

"Really good. You can come check them out if you want. I still have to do some light editing, but overall, I think they're good to go."

I dried my hands on the towel, pulled the chair out beside her, and sat down. She turned the computer so I could see the screen and started clicking through images.

While checking out my shirtless friends wasn't something I enjoyed doing, I couldn't take my eyes off of the screen. The photos were stunning, and Kensy had done an outstanding job capturing the guys smiling and laughing. There were a few serious images for each guy, but for the most part, they were all true to who we were—goofy, silly firefighters that had fun and loved our family at the firehouse.

There were a few photos she had gotten of each of the platoons, as well as a large group one with both of the platoons and the Battalion Chief included. It seemed she averaged around 10-15 photos of each guy, but suddenly her body tensed next to mine as she got to mine.

I watched as picture after picture passed the screen and noticed that there were easily 75 photos of me by myself. I had felt the shift between us earlier when she started shooting and thought maybe it was just me imagining it. But the few shots she got of me when I wasn't looking confirmed that she was just as pulled into this as I was.

"Those are great photos," I said, breaking the silence.

"Thank you." Her voice was quiet, barely above a whisper.

Her fingers hovered slightly over the mouse as if she was

afraid to keep going. I could tell that there were more photos, but she stopped clicking.

"That's it," she lied, swallowing so hard I could hear it.

"Are you sure about that?" I asked, my voice low as my hand reached over and cupped hers so she couldn't move it away from the mouse.

Her breath hitched in her throat as her body froze beneath mine.

"Show me the rest, Kensy."

"That's all there is."

"You're a terrible liar, and you know it. Show me."

She pulled her lower lip in between her teeth and chewed it nervously.

"Show me, Kensy."

Her name felt like whiskey on my lips, and I wanted to get drunk on her.

"I shouldn't."

"Why not?"

She turned and looked at me, her green eyes blazing beneath her dark lashes.

"Because they weren't part of what I was hired to do."

I clicked my tongue against the roof of my mouth while debating how to respond.

"So, they're more for your *personal* collection?"

Red immediately washed over her face as she tried to pull her hand from beneath mine.

"Is that what they're for, Kensy? Your personal collection of photos?"

She shook her head, trying to look away.

Without thinking it through, I reached over and placed my finger beneath her chin, bringing her face back toward mine.

Her eyes were wild as they searched mine, looking for an answer to a question she refused to ask.

"I want to see them, Kensy. I want to see what you're so desperate to hide from me and why. Show me, or I'll look through them myself."

I could feel the heat coming off of her body as we continued to touch. There was no way in hell she wasn't feeling this too. Suddenly, she jerked her hand out from beneath mine and pulled it to her chest.

"Be my guest." She pushed her chair back and walked away, breaking the spell I felt I was under.

I could hear her behind me in the kitchen, so I knew that she wasn't mad at me for pushing; she was just too embarrassed to sit here while I looked at them. She also didn't take her laptop or close out the files so I couldn't see them, so I figured this was her way of giving me what I asked for.

I pulled the computer toward me and moved the mouse as I clicked through the first photos. They weren't bad, just me climbing down the ladder—which, by the way—made the muscles in my back and forearms look fucking amazing. It wasn't that I was being cocky about how I looked, but more so that she'd captured the perfect angles to enhance and highlight them.

The next photo stopped me in my tracks as I stared at a zoomed-in image of my ass in my turnout gear. I glanced over my shoulder to find her standing by the sink, hiding her face as she saw which picture I had stopped on.

I decided to give her a break and keep going through the rest of the photos. There were a handful of profile shots that I considered buying from her because my mom would lose her shit if she saw those and didn't have them framed on her mantle at home. But overall, they weren't bad. It wasn't like she'd snuck into the back and snapped pictures of me changing back into the jeans and t-shirt I was currently wearing.

But I also couldn't deny that there was a reason Kensy had so many more photos of me than she did of anyone else. Plus the butt shot—I was the only one who had one of those.

My heart hammered in my chest as I thought about what to do. Part of me knew that I couldn't act on whatever this was between us, but the bigger part—AKA my cock— didn't give a flying fuck. And unfortunately, he spoke a lot louder than the sane part of me did.

I pushed away from the table and crossed the room in a few strides until I was standing right in front of Kensy. I pinned her against the counter, my leg firmly pressed in between hers while my hands gripped the sink behind her to keep from touching her.

"You took a picture of my ass," I blurted out, unsure why I decided to start there.

She nodded, chewing her damn lip again as her green eyes wandered everywhere but on me.

"Why?"

Her breathing was heavier as I stood so close to her, invading her space.

"Why, Kensy?" I repeated, a slight growl in my voice.

Finally, she looked up and locked eyes with me.

"Because I like it."

"Fuck," I growled.

I reached up and grabbed the back of her head, pulling her into me as my mouth crashed down on hers. A whimper escaped her lips as her hands wrapped around my neck.

Her lips parted, allowing my tongue to explore her as she deepened the kiss. My cock hardened immediately, the strain of it against my jeans evident as she moaned when I pushed into her. I let go of her head, my hands roaming down her body, loving the way she reacted to every touch.

She pushed away from the sink, moving me with her as she scratched her hands down my chest and wrapped her legs around my waist. I grabbed her ass, holding her against my cock as we both moaned into the kiss that we refused to break.

I kneaded the soft, plush flesh of her butt with both hands, desperate to get her out of those shorts and eat her sweet pussy. They were short enough that I could move the fabric to the side enough to feel her lace thong underneath.

Fuck. Me.

"You're killing me," I groaned, finally breaking the kiss. "You're wearing a fucking thong under those shorts?"

She giggled and started grinding against my hips, looking for the friction her body was craving.

"We shouldn't be doing this," I admitted, though I couldn't care less at the moment.

"Then why can't we stop?" she asked, leaning in and running her tongue up my neck before nibbling on my ear. "I don't want you to stop touching me, Jack. In fact, I want you to touch me more."

I closed my eyes and tried to steady my breathing so I didn't blow my load before she even touched me.

"Where, Kensy?"

"Everywhere," she panted, taking my hand off of her ass and moving it around to cup her breast. "I want you to touch me everywhere. Make me come."

That was it—the word that could detonate the bomb ticking inside of me.

"Fuck," I growled again, leading us straight to my bedroom while she stayed wrapped around my waist.

Eighteen
Kensy

This was the first time I'd really been in Jack's room, other than when I snuck in to drop off his laundry, as he tossed me onto the bed and looked at me like he was a hungry lion and I was his prey. And honestly—there was nothing I wanted more right now than for Jack to eat me.

"Shorts off," he demanded, standing in front of me while kicking off his shoes and undoing his belt.

I grinned and hooked my thumbs into the waistband before pulling them down my body and tossing them to the floor.

"Panties too?" I asked, ready to remove whatever I needed to get this party started.

He shook his head.

"No, leave those on for now."

I watched as he reached behind him and pulled his shirt up and over his head, the defined line of muscles on his body making me desperate to reach out and lick him.

"This comes off too," he said, standing in front of me wearing just his jeans that were hanging low on his hips as he lifted the bottom of my tank top and started lifting it over my head.

The air was cold from the air conditioner, immediately hardening my nipples.

"No fucking bra," he muttered, licking his lips as his eyes traveled over my body.

"I wanted to be comfortable," I lied.

"You're going to be the death of me." It wasn't the first time he'd said that, and I was beginning to like the effect I was having on him.

"As long as you touch me first," I said, practically begging him to relieve this ache building between my thighs.

"Don't you worry, baby. I'm going to make you come so hard you'll never want to come for anyone else again."

Before I could say anything else, he climbed up on the bed, pushed my legs apart, and nestled himself in between them. I closed my eyes and felt his fingers trail along the inside of my thigh, inching painfully close to my lips before moving and going down the other side. He repeated the same thing on the other side, driving me wild as he continued to tease me without giving me what I needed.

"Jack," I whined, squirming beneath him to try to force his hand where I wanted it.

He chuckled and continued his slow torture back up my thigh, pausing for a second to push my panties to the side before rubbing a finger along my slit. I was already wet for him, ready to be touched.

I moaned, arching my back as he pushed it inside. My nipples hardened more as I caressed my breasts with my hands while he slid another finger into me.

"Ahhh," I cried out, spreading my legs even further. "YES!"

"I told you, baby, I'm going to make you feel really good. But you don't get to touch yourself until I say so."

He reached up and pushed my hands away while he positioned himself against my body. While his fingers continued to fuck me, he drew a pebbled nipple into his mouth and sucked hard. The combination of pain and pleasure was intoxicating, making me even wetter. I felt the tingle start to build along my spine, knowing that I was getting close to orgasm.

"Right there," I moaned, digging my fingers into his hair and gently pulling.

I moved my hips, trying to get the friction I needed with his palm against my clit before he pulled away. He released one nipple, then sucked on the other while I tried to position myself against him to get off.

"I'll let you come when it's time," he said, letting my nipple pop out of his mouth.

"JACK!" I protested, already feeling like I was going to explode.

"Relax, I promise you'll come, Kensy. Just enjoy the way I touch your body. How my tongue feels on your skin and the way my fingers stretch you as they get you ready to take my cock."

I closed my eyes and did as he asked, picturing everything he was saying.

"Do you want that, baby? Do you want my dick inside of you? Do you want to ride me until I come inside of you? Or do you want me to fuck you senseless? Do you want it hard, my dick pounding into that tight pussy of yours?

Fucking you so good you won't be able to walk right for days. Is that what you want, Kensy?"

He knew his dirty talk was turning me on, but I couldn't focus to answer him. I wanted all of those things and more. I wanted to take him down my throat and suck him dry, but I also wanted to feel him deep inside as he rearranged my organs in the best way possible.

"I want it, Jack. I want your cock."

"Good girl," he whispered, giving each nipple a final kiss before moving down my body, planting kisses along the way.

Finally, I felt his hot breath on my clit and nearly came off the bed when he flicked his tongue repeatedly against it.

"HOLY. FUCKING. SHIT!"

I could feel the vibration of his chuckle against my thighs before he pressed in further and sucked my clit until I came on his face. My legs trembled against him, demanding to shut even though he firmly kept them open. I felt the spasms as his tongue and fingers worked their magic, drawing every last bit of my orgasm out of me.

Once I was done, I laid limp on the bed, unable to move if I wanted to.

He moved beside me and licked his lips, showing me the evidence of my arousal on his face before casually wiping it away with his hand.

"You taste just like I thought you would," he said quietly, brushing a strand of hair out of my face.

"Yeah?" I replied, using everything I had in me to get the words out.

"Mmm hmm. And I lied earlier. Those were the *second-best* tacos I've ever had. This is now officially the best," he teased as his hand reached down and caressed my overly sensitive pussy.

"Well, I'm glad you like *my taco*," I teased, enjoying the feel of his body next to mine. "I still want that cock, though."

"Your wish is my command."

He got up and unbuttoned his jeans, tossing them to the floor before retrieving a condom from his nightstand. He was standing there wearing nothing but a pair of black boxer briefs that did nothing to hide the bulging erection underneath. No wonder I thought that thing was a flashlight—it was HUGE. I propped myself up on my elbows to enjoy the show.

I wasn't a virgin and had been with a few guys before now, but I had never been with someone as well-endowed as Jack, which made me start to panic that maybe he was too big.

"Don't worry, it'll fit," he laughed, reading the thoughts that must have been flashing across my face.

He slowly pulled his briefs down, his erection springing free and jutting up to his stomach as he grabbed it with one hand and stroked while I watched.

My mouth watered at the sight, desperately wanting to take him inside and suck it like a lollipop.

"Is this what you want?" he asked, stepping closer as I got on all fours and crawled across the bed to him.

I nodded and locked eyes with him as I reached out and grabbed it, wrapping my hand tightly around his shaft. I stroked him slowly, watching his face as he responded to my touch. His eyes closed, and his head fell back while his lips parted, my name a whisper on them.

I leaned forward, taking a moment to appreciate the cock in front of me and the drops of precum that glistened on the tip before I took him into my mouth. My jaws were tight but loosened up quickly as I adjusted to his size and took him as deep into my throat as possible. I heard him moan as his hands dug into my hair, gently pulling every time I sucked.

My hands worked the length of him that I couldn't fit in my mouth, and soon, I'd created a rhythm that had him clenching his butt cheeks to keep from coming.

"No," he said sternly, his words strangled in his throat. "While I'd love to come down this beautiful throat of yours, I'm not doing this without being inside of you first."

He slowly pulled away, giving me a pointed look when I tried to suck harder before he finally freed himself.

"You give wonderful head, Kensy, but I want to feel that pussy wrapped around my cock as I pound into it—got it?"

I nodded, eager and ready for him to follow through on his promise.

"How do you want it?" he asked, tearing the condom wrapper with his teeth before sheathing himself.

"I don't care as long as you fuck me."

His blue eyes darkened as he grabbed me and kissed my lips roughly before spinning me around.

"On your hands and knees," he instructed, pointing to the center of the bed.

I crawled back to where I was before and did as instructed. The bed dipped a few seconds later from his weight as he climbed up behind me.

"Are you ready, baby?" he asked, sticking his hand between my thighs and stroking a finger through my folds. "Fuck yeah, you're ready. So wet for me."

I spread my legs further and popped my ass up, still wearing my thong. I could tell he liked it because he did that primal growl thing before he spanked my ass and pushed the tip of his cock inside.

I gasped, and my head hung forward as I tried to get used to the burning sensation as he stretched me wider than I imagined.

"You okay?"

I nodded, unable to speak as my body quickly adjusted to him while he slowly slid in further.

His fingers tightly gripped my hips, holding me in place until he was fully seated inside of me. He was still, not moving an inch, as my pussy relaxed and welcomed his cock.

I'd never felt this full before in my life, and suddenly, I wasn't sure if anything else would ever be this satisfying again. I wanted to feel him and started to slowly move my hips, pushing him against my walls.

"Fuck, baby, you're gonna make me come right away if you don't stop that," he warned.

"I'm sorry, I just want to feel you. It feels so good," I moaned.

"You feel good too. Too good. You make me want to blow my load, and I haven't even fucked you yet."

"I want you to fuck me, Jack. Please… I want you to pound into me like you promised."

"Give me a minute, baby. Then I'll give it to you."

The ache between my thighs was already starting to build again, so I reached down and started rubbing my clit when his hand jerked down and stopped me.

"It's my job to make you come," he warned. "No touching unless I tell you to."

"Okay, then make me come," I bit back, starting to grind my hips against him.

"Fuck, Kensy," he breathed, then did exactly as I asked.

He gripped my hips and held me in place as he thrust hard into me, then pulled all the way out before pounding back into me. It was hard and rough and felt fan-fucking-tastic, making my toes curl as I screamed his name at the top of my lungs while my orgasm built to a new level.

Every time he slammed inside of me felt like heaven, and when he spanked my ass, it drove me over the edge. I was on the verge of crying from how good it felt when he suddenly stopped pulling out and decided to jackhammer me instead. He reached down and used two fingers to spread my lips while he rubbed my clit with his middle finger, all while fucking me as hard as he could and sending my body into oblivion.

"I'm coming!" I shouted, my body trembling as I spasmed against his fingers while his cock twitched inside me as he came right behind me.

I collapsed on the bed, no longer able to hold myself up, smiling when I felt his body come crashing down with mine. We laid there for a few minutes with his cock still inside me while his fingers lazily trailed across the sore skin on my ass where he had focused on spanking me.

A few minutes later, he got up and dealt with the condom while I laid there, wondering how I would ever go back to regular sex again now that I'd just had mind-blowing sex with my best friend's brother.

Nineteen
Capshaw

Never in a million years did I ever imagine that Kensy would be lying naked in my bed, fast asleep after spending the whole night fucking her senseless. When we first started, I told myself that it would only be one time—just enough to get her out of my system and move on. A friendly fuck between friends.

But the problem was that I didn't know just how fucking good Kensy was going to be, and once I had a taste of her, there was no going back. Soon it was just a second round to get both of us our fills and then we'd stop. Then I thought for sure the third time would be the charm. But after the sixth round, I'd run out of condoms, and Kensy was knocked out cold in my bed.

I'd gotten up around two in the morning for a glass of water and decided to take a few minutes to think about what had happened. Even though I tried to tell myself there were a million reasons why something shouldn't happen between us, I couldn't get my heart or my dick to agree with me— which was why I ended up making a last-minute trip to the gas station for more condoms when she woke up a few hours later, ready for another round.

Kensy wasn't like anyone I'd ever met before. She was fun, smart, beautiful, ambitious, and she didn't take no for an answer—like when I told her my cock needed a break to reset and she insisted on sucking it back to life. See what I mean?

But I still had no idea how she felt about any of this, and while last night was fun and mind-blowing to say the least, that didn't mean that she was ready to get on board with being something more than just friends. We'd already crossed that line so there was no going back, but I didn't know what that made us now.

I'd gone back to bed around four in the morning and tried to sleep, but knowing that her naked body was merely inches away from mine kept me up and struggling not to touch her. Finally, around six, she rolled over and brushed the hair out of her eyes as she smiled at me.

"Good morning."

"Good morning," I replied, my hand reaching out to brush against her thigh without warning.

Her legs immediately parted, and before I knew it, we were going at it again. By the time we both came up for air, it was after eight, and our stomachs were growling. I sent Kensy to shower and clean up while I worked on breakfast. It was a simple meal of eggs and sausage, but there wasn't much to work with, given that I needed to go grocery shopping today.

As soon as the food was ready, Kensy came in wearing nothing but a loose-fitting t-shirt and a pair of black boy short panties underneath. Her hair was wet and smelled like the tropical shampoo she used.

"Breakfast is ready and the coffee will be done in a minute," I said as I set a plate of food down in front of her on the table.

"Thank you, it smells delicious."

I joined her a few minutes later, unable to take my eyes off of her. I sighed heavily, frustrated with myself for already being so hard up on someone when I didn't know if they felt the same way.

I cut into the sausage with my fork and popped a bite into my mouth while she took a sip of her coffee. The silence was killing me, but I didn't want to come off too strong and scare her away by asking her how she felt about what happened between us last night.

She pierced her sausage link with her fork and parted her lips as she lifted it to her mouth. The way she looked reminded me of last night when she sucked my cock. I slammed my hand down on the table, rattling the plates as her eyes widened in surprise.

"Are you okay?" she asked, setting her fork down and studying me.

"Yeah, sorry." I exhaled heavily and ran my hand down my face. "I'm just a little off this morning."

She nodded as if that told her something and lowered her hands to her lap.

"Is this about what happened last night?" she asked, her voice quiet.

I rubbed my lips together, unsure of how to answer.

Instead, I nodded.

"I see." She blinked quickly as tears started to pool in her eyes. "I'm sorry that you regret what happened, Jack. I assure you it won't happen again."

She pushed away from the table and stood up. My mind was spinning as it struggled to process the words she said. I got up and grabbed her arm before she could leave.

"Wait—what?"

"I said it won't happen again. I didn't mean to cross that line and make you feel uncomfortable. I can start looking for a new place today as well."

I shook my head, desperate to clear the fog.

"No, Kensy," I sighed. "That's not at all what I'm bothered by this morning. I don't regret what happened between us last night."

"You don't?"

"No." I relaxed my grip on her arm once I knew she wasn't going to keep trying to run away. "I very much enjoyed what happened last night."

"Then what's the problem?" she asked, folding her arms over her chest.

"I don't know," I exhaled. "I guess the problem is that something changed for me last night, and I realized that I might be falling for you."

Her eyes widened at my admission.

"You might be falling for me?" she repeated quietly with a large amount of uncertainty.

I nodded.

"And I've been stressed because I don't know how you feel about last night, and I didn't want to be the only one stuck out here, having all of these feelings and shit."

"Feelings and shit?" she giggled, covering her mouth with her hand. "You're so romantic."

"You know what I mean," I teased, rolling my eyes as I nudged her with my shoulder.

"Well, in that case, I might be having feelings and shit too." Her cheeks blushed that adorable shade of pink again and I wished I could bottle it up and keep it forever.

My eyebrows rose as I processed what she was saying.

"You have feelings for me? And I have feelings for you?" I confirmed.

"And shit," she added, pulling her bottom lip between her teeth as she grinned.

I grabbed her, pulling her into my chest as I tickled her sides.

"Well then, it's settled. We have feelings and shit for each other."

She sighed heavily, allowing her body to relax into mine.

After breakfast, Kensy worked on editing the photos she didn't get around to last night because we were fucking like bunnies while I cleaned out the garage. It had been driving me nuts for months, and boxes were piled up with things that needed to be donated. By lunchtime, I'd gone in to find Kensy still working, so I took advantage of the time and ran some errands.

I knew I needed to get groceries, but I wasn't sure what Kensy needed, so I waited for her to finish up so we could go together. It felt like such a *couple* thing to do, but technically that's what we were now.

I finished up the last few things that I needed to get done and then texted her to see if she wanted to go grocery shopping with me. She confirmed she had just wrapped up and needed a break. I parked in the driveway and waited for her to climb in before we headed to the store.

Part of me felt nervous that people in town would see us together and suspect that something had happened, but then part of me didn't care. While I knew that I still needed to tell Lia—or see if Kensy wanted to—no one else's opinion mattered to me. I had been known as the bachelor of Beaumont Creek for so long that everyone was used to seeing me with a different woman. Now that they knew Kensy was living with me, it wouldn't be a huge surprise that we'd go shopping together.

But still, even though I tried to assure myself that everything was fine and that I didn't care what they thought about us, I found myself getting Kensy her own shopping cart before grabbing one of my own. She gave me a weird look, but I tried to ignore it as I headed for the meat section because, obviously, meat fixes everything.

I went up and down the aisles, grabbing the items I needed while Kensy spent most of her time in the produce section. I knew she liked to eat healthily and cooked often, which made me second guess the stack of frozen pizzas sitting in my cart. If she could make better choices, so could I.

I grumbled under my breath and headed back to the freezer section to return them when I rounded the corner and ran into Lia.

"Hey! What are you doing here?" she asked, pulling me in for a hug.

"Grocery shopping," I replied, pointing to my half-empty cart. "It's what most people do here."

"Smart ass," she muttered, smacking my arm with the little wallet thing attached to her wrist by a strap. "I just thought it was weird that you and Kensy are both here. I just ran into her when I came in."

"Why is it weird? Kensy eats food too."

Her brows furrowed as she studied me. I was being defensive and knew it.

"Yeah… but since she lives with you, I figured you guys would shop *together*."

"Why would we be together? Who said we were?"

She pulled her head back and gave me a quizzical look.

"What's wrong with you? Did you eat bad mushrooms again?"

"Nothing," I lied. "I'm just tired."

"Mmm hmm." She folded her arms and continued to study me. "That's not it."

"Yes it is. And if you'll excuse me, I need to finish up my shopping so I can go home and take a nap."

She looked down at her watch and then back up at me.

"It's 4:30. You don't nap, let alone this late. Should I call mom? Are you dying or something?"

I rolled my eyes, my irritation growing thicker.

"Really, Lia? Dying?"

"You're the one who's being all weird. How am I supposed to know what's wrong with you?"

"Aren't you the one who's going to med school? What are they teaching you there anyway?"

Now it was her turn to roll her eyes.

"Hey, there you are," Kensy said, coming around the corner with her shopping cart filled to the top. "I was looking for you."

"Me or Lia?" I asked, confused as I pointed between my sister and me.

"You…"

"He's being weird, isn't he?" Lia asked Kensy, ignoring the fact that I was still standing right there.

"A little bit," Kensy agreed. "He didn't sleep well last night, so he might just be tired."

"That's what he said, but it seems like it's more than that. Did he eat any mushrooms?"

"Not that I know of. Why?"

"Well, one time he found these mush—"

"Can we please not tell that story today?" I interrupted, rubbing my temples as a headache started building behind my eyes.

"Why not? I want to hear it," Kensy objected.

"Trust me, you don't," I assured her.

"You do," Lia said smugly, giving me a look. "One time Jack stayed the night with our grandparents and found some mushrooms in the kitchen. He was hungry because he didn't like the dinner they had made the night before, so he snuck some of the mushrooms and hid in his bedroom to eat them. The only problem was that they were my grandpa's, and well, they weren't the kind of mushrooms kids should be eating. No one knew about it until they found him in his closet, hugging his new best friend, the broom."

"Oh my gosh!" Kensy covered her mouth with her hands. "How old was he?"

"I don't remember. Eleven, twelve? I was too young to remember it, but my family loves telling the story."

"Well, no, he hasn't had any mushrooms, but I'll be sure to watch him now that I know," Kensy teased and then turned to me. "These ones are safe."

I tried to fight the smile that threatened to spread across my cheeks as she lifted a pack of portabella mushrooms from her cart and showed me.

"Funny," I teased. "But I do need to finish my shopping, so if you two will excuse me."

"I'm actually heading to mom's, so I gotta run. Call me later and we'll do Tipsy Taquito, Kens. Bye, booger face," Lia said, leaning in to kiss my cheek.

"Will do," Kensy called after her as she sauntered down the aisle.

"So, mushrooms?"

"It was a long time ago," I said with a laugh. "Did you get everything you need?"

"Yeah, I was just going to check out the wine section, and then I'm done. You?"

She looked into my cart and frowned when it had nothing but frozen food, including the pizzas I was headed to put back.

"Don't judge. I get burnt out on cooking, so sometimes it's easier to throw something in the oven and let it do all of the work."

"I'm not judging, but how about a compromise?"

"Okay?"

"Since you're letting me stay with you and refuse to take any money for rent, how about I cook all of the meals while I'm home?"

"You don't have to do that, Kensy, but thank you. I don't mind eating this stuff."

"I mind," she insisted, grabbing a handful of items from my cart and carrying them down the aisle as she looked through the freezer doors to see where they went. "This stuff isn't good for you, Jack. You should eat better. Plus, I'm cooking for myself anyway; it's not that hard to make extra and feed both of us."

"I don't like the idea of you cooking all the time for me."

She spun around and planted her hands on her hips as she stared at me.

"Okay, then how about this—we cook together. I'll come up with the menu each week and make sure we have all of the ingredients that we need, but we prepare the meals together when you're home."

I pulled my mouth to the side as I thought about it.

"Alright, that I can do. But how do you know how to cook all of this stuff anyway?" I asked, looking in her cart at the wide variety of foods she'd picked.

"Oh, that's easy. I'm OBSESSED with cooking shows and soak up everything I see. If I see someone make something once, I can usually recreate it."

"Good to know," I joked. "The only thing I make that's decent is apple pie."

"Well then, looks like that's what we're having for dessert tonight."

She winked over her shoulder before bending down to put some of the frozen hot wings back. I couldn't help but check out her ass as the denim shorts pulled tightly across it.

"I was thinking maybe I want something else for dessert…."

She blushed as I brushed past her and whispered, "your pussy."

Twenty
Kensy

Jack was back on shift Sunday, which was super convenient given that Bella was coming over to do boudoir photos, and I wasn't ready to be around him in front of other people yet. I knew that I was an open book with my face giving me away, so the last thing I needed was Bella or Lia asking me what was going on with him since Lia was coming to help Bella with her hair and make up.

I'd gotten the room ready early and moved a few things out of the way so I wouldn't have to edit them out of the photos later. The curtains were pulled back, allowing the natural light to seep through the sheers. It was the perfect setting, and I was so excited to do her photos in this room.

I had my camera set up on a tripod, angled at the bed to get the shots that I knew I wanted when I heard the doorbell. I rushed off to answer the door, feeling slightly nervous about how comfortable I felt in Jack's house—as if it were my own. I hadn't felt like anywhere was home since I lived with my dad, so this was new territory for me, and I wasn't sure what to do with all the emotions bubbling up inside.

"Hello!" I greeted as I opened the door and stepped to the side to let the girls in. Bella looked beautiful already, her olive-toned complexion making me jealous of her natural beauty.

Lia came in behind her with a duffle bag on her shoulder and two iced coffees.

"Here, I brought coffee," she said with a smile, extending one to me.

"You are the best," I squealed, taking it as I closed the door with my bare foot and followed them into the living room. "I have the bedroom set up, but let me know if there are other photos you want as well."

"I think just the bedroom would be good. I might feel weird wearing sexy lingerie on Capshaw's couch," Bella giggled.

I felt my cheeks burn as I blushed and hoped the iced coffee would cool me off. I took a long sip and tried not to let the memories of me and Jack fucking on the couch last night before bed come to the surface.

"No problem, bedroom it is," I replied with a little too much enthusiasm. I felt Lia's eyes on me but refused to look at her. "Did you bring the outfits you wanted to wear?" It was a stupid question, given that Bella had a tote bag with pink lace peaking out of the top, but I needed to pull the attention away from me and why I was acting so strange.

"I did, plus a few extras just in case I don't like some of the ones I picked. I tried everything on last night but felt like some of them made me look terrible, so I wasn't sure I wanted to use those after all."

"You look amazing in everything you wear," Lia said, rolling her eyes as she pressed the straw to her lips and took a drink. "Plus, you can add or delete things from your portfolio later if you no longer like it. But this is a surefire way to get that agency's attention."

"Which agency is it again?" I asked, hating that I had already forgotten some of the details she'd told me when we first talked about doing this.

"It's Prestige. They're super hard to get noticed by, but they're also one of the biggest agencies and have the best reputation."

"Well then, let's get working on giving them something they can't resist." I wiggled my eyebrows and motioned for them to follow me.

Bella went to the bathroom to get changed while I played with the camera settings and listened to Lia tell me about her newest crush on some guy she had a class with.

"What happened with Joseph?" I asked, glancing up at her before I went back to the camera settings.

"It turned out that he was hot, but that was about it. He was soooo dull, and literally, all we talked about during our *study session* was prescription drugs and their possible side effects."

I laughed and shook my head. Lia had been boy-crazy since I met her, and nothing had changed since then.

"Well, I think that was the whole point of getting together to study," I said as I took a few practice photos. "Can you come sit down so I can see if I've got this right?"

She set her iced coffee on the dresser and climbed up on the bed, posing dramatically as I clicked the remote. While I enjoyed pressing the shutter button and being in the moment, I also knew that I worked better when I didn't have to be behind the camera and could help direct Bella where I wanted her to be and how I wanted her to pose.

"I know, but it was so boring. The least he could have done was give me a quick study break with a hot make-out session," Lia grumbled, letting her hair fall down her back as she arched it and looked up at the ceiling.

"Who had a hot make-out session?" Bella asked, walking into the room. "Also—that pose is hot as fuck, Lia."

"It is, isn't it?" I confirmed, studying her position so I could put Bella into it next. "You look pretty hot too, Bella. I would buy that lingerie just based on how good you look wearing it."

"Thanks." She smiled as her fingers trailed over the delicate lace fabric of the bodysuit. It had a plunging neckline with a thin strap that tied behind her neck. She turned around to give us the full view, showing off how the back dipped low, just barely covering her ass.

Lia climbed off of the bed and then smoothed the white blanket I had on top to cover the plaid print comforter. Bella took her spot and let Lia apply another coat of red lipstick before helping her get into the same position she was in a few minutes before.

Once she was ready, I got started, moving around to check different angles before I moved the tripod and captured more. While I loved doing family photography, I found that I enjoyed boudoir photography even more. Something about it pulled the creativity out of me, and I found myself posing Bella in ways I would never have imagined.

A few hours later, we were done. There had to be at least two hundred pictures to go through before I started editing, but I was confident that she was going to like what we got. How could she not—she was freaking gorgeous and rocked every single outfit she wore—even the more risqué ones that might have made me blush when she first came in because she looked that sexy.

"Did you guys want to go to The Tipsy Taquito for dinner?" Bella asked, setting her bag down on the floor by the couch after she finished getting changed. "My treat."

"That sounds delicious," Lia said. "But you're not paying for mine."

"Don't be ridiculous," Bella argued, rolling her eyes. "I'm treating as a thank you for your guys' help today. All of the hair and makeup and fixing thongs that went too far up my butt—that all deserves some margaritas and tacos."

"Thanks for the offer, but I think I'm going to—"

"No," Lia interrupted, holding her hand up to stop me.

"What?" I lifted my shoulders and let them fall, genuinely confused by what her problem was with me not going.

"You're coming with us, Kens. I know that you're worried about money, but I've got you. We haven't gone out in forever and need to catch up on some juicy gossip."

I chewed the inside of my cheek and debated giving in and going. My checking account was still low since I was still waiting for the sleazy landlord to process the refund he owed me, but I could probably afford to splurge a little bit tonight. Payday was coming up, I would just have to be smart with my money for another week or so.

"Fine," I sighed. "But the gossip better be good."

Twenty-One

Kensy

"I don't know who it is, but I know that Kensy is hooking up with someone," Lia blurted out, twirling her straw in her margarita as Bella's head whipped around to look at me.

"What?! Are you hooking up with someone? Who is it?"

I swallowed hard, trying to keep myself calm. When Lia said we needed to catch up on juicy gossip, I didn't expect her to mean mine.

"I'm not," I lied. I dipped a tortilla chip in the salsa and shoved it into my mouth.

"Bullshit, I can tell that you are," Lia said, shaking her finger in my direction.

"How?" Bella asked, looking at her before turning back to study me.

"One, I know Kensy, and she gets super nervous every time I mention it, which means I'm right. She's a terrible liar—always has been. Two, she's been more relaxed today, like she got a good pounding—if you know what I mean."

I cringed, wondering if she would still say that if she knew that it was her brother who had been pounding me.

"So spill it. Who are you fucking?" Lia asked, giving me a pointed look.

I was about to answer and deny that I was screwing anyone when the young, very attractive server interrupted us to deliver our food.

"Taco plate with an extra side of guacamole?" he asked, looking between us.

"Oh my God, yes, that's mine," I said breathlessly, making a fool of myself as my cheeks tinted pink with embarrassment.

His brows pulled down as he handed me my plate, then grabbed the next one off the tray and gave it to Lia. The girls watched me with spiked curiosity until he left.

"Is *that* the guy you're doing? Are you like getting free tacos in exchange for sex?" Lia asked in a hushed tone.

"What?" I choked, my bite nearly going down the wrong way and lodging in my throat. "Why on earth would you assume that I would be trading sex for tacos?"

She shrugged and took a bite of hers.

"I don't know. I would do it. Their tacos are delicious and I know how much you love guacamole. Seems like a fair deal."

My eyes bulged as I stared at my best friend and wondered what in the world was wrong with her.

"No, Lia, I'm not prostituting myself for tacos and guacamole."

"I wouldn't judge you if you did." She winked and took another bite.

"Okay, so you're not doing it with that guy," Bella said cautiously, not bothering to touch her food yet. "So, who are you doing it with?"

I scooped some guacamole onto a chip and thought about how to answer that. It wasn't like Jack and I had stopped to talk about when we would tell people about us—especially Lia. We had only agreed that something was there, and we wanted to explore it. Plus, it wasn't like we could hide it forever. Eventually, people were going to figure it out.

I rubbed my lips together and took a deep breath, studying the green mountain of deliciousness piled on top of the chip that would soon break from the weight of the guacamole it was trying to hold.

"I can't say," I replied easily before taking a bite and wiping my mouth.

"So you *are* sleeping with someone," Bella squealed, clapping her hands.

"Maybe…."

"You can't tell us you're screwing someone and then not tell us who it is," Lia objected, her brows furrowed. "We want all of the details—like if he's hung like a horse, how good is he on a scale of 1-10, does he know how to eat pu—"

"I'm going to stop you right there," I exclaimed. "*You* do not want me to give you those details."

Lia's face shifted from frustrated to confused to realization within seconds.

"You've got to be fucking kidding me."

I flinched at the anger in her voice as Bella looked between us, not yet catching what was happening.

"I didn't mean for it to happen," I said softly, searching her eyes for the Lia I knew instead of the angry beast-looking one who looked like she wanted to reach across the table and strangle me. "I'm sorry, Lia."

"Wait, what's going on?" Bella asked though it was met with silence as Lia continued to stare me down with her fork gripped tightly in her fist. "Oh, shit! You're doing Capshaw?"

I pulled my eyes away from Lia to look at Bella and nodded.

"Holy shit!" she squealed, squirming in her seat beside Lia. "I know you're super pissed about this, Lia, but come on, you had to have seen this coming."

"Why would I see this coming?" Lia asked, turning her anger to Bella.

"How could you not? Even *I* can feel the chemistry between them the few times I've been around both of them. And now they're living together. I don't know why I didn't figure it out sooner," she laughed, then her eyes widened. "Oh my GOD! That's why you blushed so bad earlier when I said I didn't want to sit in my lingerie on Capshaw's couch—you guys did it there, didn't you?"

The color in my face drained as Lia turned and glared at me again, this time the vein in her forehead making an appearance.

"Maybe we should talk about something else?" I offered quietly, pulling my gaze away from Lia's.

"Oh hell, no," Lia muttered. "You're not getting off that easy."

"It seems like maybe she is," Bella joked. "I mean, you said yourself that she seemed more relaxed lately. Obviously your brother is getting her off pretty goo—"

"Shut your mouth," Lia snapped, closing her eyes and rubbing her temples. "I can't take this right now. This was supposed to be fun, juicy gossip about someone *other than* my brother."

"I'm sorry, Lia. We didn't mean for it to happen."

"Is it going to continue to happen?" she asked, opening her eyes to look at me.

I nodded.

"I like him. A lot. I can't explain it, but there's something between us that I've never felt before, and I want to see where it goes."

"And how does he feel?" she questioned.

I shrugged, uncomfortable to be answering for him.

"I think he feels the same way. It's all so new, and we haven't had much time to sit down and discuss what it means."

"How long has it been going on?" Lia asked, her shoulders finally relaxing a little.

"Only a few days," I rushed out. "Since Friday night."

"That's why he was acting so weird when I ran into you guys at the store yesterday."

"Yeah, plus he really didn't get much sleep—but that wasn't all because of me."

She arched an eyebrow, and I couldn't help the giggle that escaped from me. The corners of her lips started to curl up into a smile, allowing me to relax.

"Alright, now that you're not being all *murdery,* can she give us the details of what happened, when it happened, and how it happened?" Bella asked Lia, pressing her hands in front of her.

"I don't want *all* of the details—keep it to where I can actually look my brother in the eye the next time I see him."

"Deal," I laughed. "There's not much to tell. I don't really know when it started. There was some flirting at work, but it was always so subtle that I didn't know if it was real or if I had just imagined it. Then after I moved in with him, things just moved quickly after that. He was on shift the first two days I was there, and then there was that nasty storm the first night he was off shift. The power got knocked out, and I was getting a drink of water when he came into the kitchen and startled me. We were looking for flashlights together when I accidentally mistook his—you know—for one."

I cringed when Lia closed her eyes and leaned back against the booth while Bella burst into laughter.

"You thought his dick was a flashlight," she whispered, leaning across the table toward me.

I nodded and laughed.

"I kept pulling on it and didn't realize it was him until he made this strangled noise and told me. I felt so stupid after that."

"So it's," Bella paused and held her hand up to shield Lia from seeing her as she mouthed the word "big" to me.

"Very," I confirmed.

"Oh my God!" Bella stomped her feet excitedly under the table.

"Then he offered to *light up the night* if I needed him to," I whispered back behind my hand, even though I knew Lia could hear us.

"Ewww. Gross." She scrunched her face, making Bella and me laugh harder.

"I cannot believe you thought it was a flashlight," Bella laughed, forking a piece of lettuce from her taco salad.

"It was big, round, hard—I mean, it fit the description."

We laughed as we ate, the energy finally shifting back to how it was before Lia found out I was fucking her brother.

Twenty-Two
Capshaw

"We can't go out to eat every time it's Jones' turn to cook," I joked as we all piled into the truck and headed for food.

"I agree, but given that none of us are willing to eat burnt macaroni, we don't have much choice," Nate said with a shrug.

I leaned back against the seat, debating on pulling my phone out to text Kensy to see how her day was. I hadn't heard from her all day but knew that she had Bella's boudoir session today and was busy. But it was already after six, and I figured she was done by now.

We parked on the street since the truck was too big to fit in the parking lot without taking up several spaces and then climbed out and headed into The Tipsy Taquito. We were eating out a lot more these days as we made a group effort to teach Jones how to cook. It backfired every time, so we tried to mix it up, so we weren't constantly eating at the same place.

The line was relatively long, with the other guys going before me while I finally gave in and texted Kensy to see how she was. Within seconds, my phone buzzed with a response from her.

Kensy: I'm good, how are you?

Me: Tired but good. Out grabbing a bite to eat with the

guys. Jones burned the mac and cheese again.

Kensy: Oh no! I'm out having dinner with Lia and Bella.

Me: Oh yeah? Where did you guys decide to go?

Kensy: The Tipsy Taquito.

I lowered my phone and immediately scanned the room, looking for her. What were the odds that we would end up at the same place at the same time? Maybe it was the universe taking pity on me because I had been obsessing all day over when I would get to see her again.

Within seconds, I spotted her red hair piled loosely on her head and smiled.

Me: Funny, me too.

Kensy: What? Where are you?

Me: In line, staring at the most beautiful woman in the entire restaurant

I was still staring at her when I saw her lift up in the booth and lock eyes with me. Her face lit up as her smile spread across her cheeks, mine mirroring hers.

She gave me a little wave before Bella and Lia turned around and spotted me. Bella had a shit-eating grin, while Lia looked like she wanted to murder me.

Kensy: Ummm… by the way… Lia knows.

Me: Is that why she looks like she wants to murder me?

Kensy: It is. She just barely released her death grip on her fork a few minutes ago.

Me: Eh, I'm not scared of her.

Kensy: I would be. She's fucking scary when she's mad.

Me: She came into this world screaming and throwing a fit, I can handle her. Don't worry.

I tucked my phone into my pocket as I stepped up to the register and placed my to-go order. After I got my receipt, I grabbed my cup and went to the soda station to fill it.

"You're fucking my best friend?" Lia asked loudly as she stood beside me.

I heard the guys snickering but didn't bother to look at them as I focused on not overfilling the cup.

"Hey, Lia, how are you?" I asked, avoiding the question as I snapped the lid on the cup and grabbed a straw from the dispenser.

"Don't act like you didn't hear me." She planted her hands on her hips and glared.

"I heard you, but it's none of your business."

"It is my business. She's my best friend, and if you hurt her, I'll—"

"You'll what, Lia?"

"You don't want to know," she huffed out. "But I guarantee that even a medical examiner won't be able to figure out what organs are what after I get done with you."

"You're overreacting."

"Am I?"

"Yes. And on top of it, you're making a scene." I lowered my voice and turned my body so the guys couldn't see what I was saying. "I know that Kensy is your best friend, but this has nothing to do with you. She's a grown woman, Lia, and I have no intention of hurting her. Believe it or not, I really like her, and I would love it if you would step back and allow us to see what this thing between us is without you interfering."

She pulled her shoulders back and sighed heavily.

"She's been through a lot, Capshaw. You need to understand that. Kensy didn't have the same childhood that we did. She experienced a lot of pain that she never should have, and I don't want to see her go through more."

"I understand. But instead of worrying that I'm out to break her heart, maybe consider that I could be the one to heal it and put it back together, Lia."

Her face softened as the anger lifted from it.

"Oh my God," she said softly. "I can't believe it."

"Believe what?"

"You love her. You've already fallen for her, haven't you?"

I opened my mouth to deny what she was saying, but the words refused to come out.

"Don't you dare tell her," I warned, hating that my sister now had a secret she could hold over me.

Twenty-Three
Kensy

"Knead the dough like this," Jack instructed from behind me as his hands guided me to do what he was asking.

I wanted to pay attention and do as he asked, but all I could focus on was his dick pressed against my ass, trapping me between him and the island as he attempted to teach me how to make an apple pie from scratch.

"There you go, pull a little harder."

My breathing got heavier as I closed my eyes and tried to ignore the way his words seemed to trigger something inside of me that made me want to jump his bones every second of the day.

"You okay?" he asked, his breath hot against my ear.

"Mmm hmm."

"You sure? Because you're rubbing your ass against my cock instead of working the dough."

"I'm sorry," I giggled. "I can't think of anything other than *you* working *me*. You feel so good against me that all I can think about is you fucking my ass and making me come."

His hands let go of mine, the dough thumping to the counter with a loud thud.

"This ass?" he asked, rubbing his hand along it, his finger caressing my asshole.

I let my head fall back and moaned.

"I would love nothing more than to fuck this beautiful ass of yours, Kensy."

He spun me around and then tossed me over his shoulder as I giggled on the way to his bedroom. He gently set me down on the bed, went to the bathroom, and returned with a bottle of lube.

I pulled my yoga pants down, laughing at the flour hand print on the back before tossing them to the floor and stripping off my panties.

"Have you done anal before?" he asked as he grabbed the back of his t-shirt and pulled it over his head.

His body got me every time, and I found myself fantasizing about him instead of answering his question. He stood before me, lifted my chin with his finger, and brought my attention back to him.

"Have you done anal before, Kensy?"

"Yes, a few times."

His jaw clenched as he reached behind me and squeezed a handful of ass hard.

"From here on, this ass is mine. No one else's, got that?"

I chewed my lower lip until he popped it free with his finger.

"Got it?"

"Yes, sir," I answered playfully, loving the way he reacted every time I did.

"On the bed," he commanded, turning to take off his jeans.

I did as he asked, taking my bra off and tossing it to the floor, now completely naked.

"Have you ever been blindfolded?" he asked.

"No, but I'm not against it."

"You sure?"

I nodded, excited to try something new with him.

He dug around in the top drawer of his dresser and then joined me on the bed with a black tie.

"I'm going to put this on you, but if at any time you want me to stop—you need to tell me. Come up with a safe word, so I know that we've reached your limits."

"A safe word?" I asked, even though I knew what he was talking about. I just couldn't think of one on the spot when my pussy was practically begging to be touched.

He nodded and sat back on his heels while he waited for me to come up with one.

"Umm… I don't know." I lifted my hands and let them fall in my lap. "Okra?"

His brows lifted as a grin spread across his face.

"Your safe word is Okra?"

I shrugged and smiled along with him.

"I mean, if you hear me yell out okra while we're doing

stuff, you'll know for sure that I'm not into it since I cannot stand okra."

"Alright, fine by me." He chuckled and motioned for me to lean forward so he could secure the tie around my eyes. He pulled it tightly, brushing my hair out of the way first.

"Is that too tight?" he asked, the bed dipping beside me as he moved around.

"Nope, it's fine."

"Alright, lie on your back and wait for me."

"Wait for you? Where are you going?" I questioned as I did as he asked.

He didn't answer, but a few minutes later I felt the bed shift beside me again as he climbed on.

I felt the warmth of his hand as it caressed my thigh, leaving goosebumps in its wake as it made its way up to my pussy. I expected to feel his fingers part me and slip inside, the way they always did but gasped when I felt the sharp sting of something cold and wet instead.

"What the hell is that?" I yelped, squirming to move away from it.

"Ice," he answered, his voice sounding distant.

I took a deep breath and tried to get used to the cold. His fingers continued to tickle my skin as he moved the ice cube around, then I felt him part my folds and slip the ice cube inside. I bolted forward, only to be greeted by his other hand gently pushing me back onto the bed.

"Trust me," he instructed before lowering his mouth to my

pussy, the warmth of his breath creating a new sensation against the cold sting of the ice cube.

I moaned as his tongue plunged deeper inside, pushing the ice cube against my walls as I tried not to squirm beneath him while his hands held my hips in place.

I panted as he continued his delicious torture until the ice cube melted and he pulled his tongue out. I wanted more. Needed more. My body was on fire, aching for the sweet release I knew he could give me.

"How are you feeling, baby?" he asked as he moved around beside me.

"Like I want to come," I panted, my hand reaching down to touch myself since he no longer was.

"You know better," he warned, moving my hand away.

"But, I need it. Please," I begged.

"You'll get it, but you have to be patient. I'm not done with you yet."

I wanted to object and tell him that he needed to let me come now, but before I could, I felt something cold slide inside of me, this time much bigger than the ice cube.

"Ahhhh," I cried out, my fingers digging into the sheets as I arched my back for me. "What is that?"

"A cucumber," he answered, pushing it in further.

My mind was hazy as I focused on the sensations coursing through me.

I panted harder, about to completely lose it as he fucked me harder with it.

"Fuck yeah," I moaned, my chest rising and falling heavily. "Fuck me, Jack!"

He did as instructed, moving it in and out of me in perfect rhythm as his thumb rubbed circles around my clit.

I pinched my eyes closed as I felt the first wave of spasms as my pussy pulsed around the cucumber, coming so hard that I thought I might pass out from it. He didn't let up with the pressure on my clit until my legs trembled and fell open to the side of me.

"Holy shit," I whimpered, feeling completely and totally spent as he reached up and took the tie off. "I can't believe you just fucked me with a cucumber." I laughed nervously as he held it up for me to see.

"It was the hottest thing I've ever seen." He winked and set it down beside him.

"That was supposed to be for the salad I was going to make for dinner tonight," I said, shaking my head.

"Salad is overrated," he mumbled as he nuzzled my breast, pulling a nipple between his teeth.

"If I had to choose between salad and that mind-blowing orgasm I just had, I'm going to choose the orgasm every time."

"Good to know. Maybe I'll start a garden and grow nothing but cucumbers."

I laughed and then gasped when he sucked my nipple harder, the sensation bordering on painful and pleasureful at the same time.

"Well, the cucumber was good, but it's nothing compared to your cock. Which, by the way, you have yet to give me."

"I know. I was making sure you came before I got to taking this sweet ass of yours—if that's still what you want?"

"It is very much so what I want. But go slowly," I warned. "While I've done it before, it was never with anyone who was packing an anaconda in between their legs, and I don't want you to rip my asshole to shreds."

"I'll go slow, I promise."

He leaned in and kissed me, caressing his thumb across my cheek in the most tender embrace.

"What's your safe word?" he asked softly, his words vibrating against my mouth.

"Okra," I whispered, getting one last kiss in before he pulled away.

"Promise me that you'll use it if you need it."

"I promise."

He climbed off the bed and held his hand out for me to join him.

"Have you ever done anal standing?" he asked.

"No," I shook my head, excited to try something new.

"You good doing it this way?"

"Yeah, of course."

His blue eyes searched my face before he grabbed me and spun me around so my back was pressed against his chest. I could feel his erection against my ass and pushed into it as the wetness started to pool between my thighs again.

I closed my eyes as his hands roamed over my breasts, squeezing and caressing them as he walked me a few steps to the bed and gently guided me forward so I was leaning over it with my ass popped in the air.

"Touch yourself," he said, his words strained. "Tell me how wet you are as you make yourself come, Kensy."

My hand slid down, my fingers immediately going to my clit and rubbing. I was so wet that I didn't have to worry about not having enough lubrication.

"How wet are you for me, baby?"

"Soaking," I moaned as I felt him squirt some lube onto my ass.

"Your pussy is so beautiful. Delicious. I don't know what I'm going to like better—fucking your sweet pussy or taking this tight ass."

"Ahhhh!" I cried out as he pressed a finger against my asshole, pushing gently as the lube helped it slide inside.

"You okay?"

"Mmm hmmm."

"Keep touching yourself, baby. I want you to make yourself come. Do that for me."

I nodded and focused on rubbing my clit the way I liked it but kept getting distracted by what he was doing to my ass. The sound of more lube squirting out made me even hornier than I was, my legs shaking as my orgasm started to build.

Soon he had two fingers pumping in and out of my ass while I rubbed myself, desperate for the release.

I was about to come—right on the verge—when I felt a third finger. It was so tight that I had no idea how his cock was going to fit in there if this was barely three of his fingers.

"Your ass is so tight, baby. I can feel you clenching every time you fight coming. Just let go, baby. Come for me, now."

And just like that, his words were my undoing. I rubbed harder, panting as I tried to hold onto the bed while my orgasm washed over me, and his fingers continued to fuck my ass.

"Fuck!" I screamed, waves of pleasure washing over me.

"That's it, baby," he encouraged, slowly pulling his fingers out once I was done. "Now you're ready for me."

I felt weak again, but knowing what was coming, I steadied my legs and let him line me up right in front of him, away from the bed.

"Safe word?" he asked as he gently pressed his hand on my back and pushed me into a downward dog position. I spread my legs slightly, giving him easier access.

"Okra."

"Use it if you need it."

I nodded though he couldn't see it because my head was down and almost touching the floor. He grabbed my wrists and pulled them back, pinning them in place behind me before I felt the silky fabric of the tie bind them together. I waited anxiously as I heard him tear open a condom. Then he squirted a massive amount of lube on my ass before lining his cock up at my entrance. Slowly, I felt his head as it pushed past the tight bundle, ignoring the burning sensation as I focused on taking deep breaths.

"You okay?" he asked, checking in constantly to make sure I was.

"Yeah," I breathed loud enough for him to hear. "Slowly," I reminded him.

His hands rubbed gently across my back, making circles on my skin while he let me adjust to him before he pushed a little bit further inside. Soon, the burning stopped and was replaced with pleasure as I felt how full I felt with him inside me.

He rocked gently into me and pulled out slightly, creating the friction I was craving. My breathing grew heavier with each thrust, desperate for him to go harder and deeper.

"I want more," I panted. "Fuck me, Jack. I can take it. Please, just fuck me."

With my hands restrained, I couldn't do anything but stand there, bent over at his mercy, and I loved every second of it. Once he knew that I was okay, he gripped my hips and started to fuck me the way I wanted him to. Fast, hard, and thoroughly until he came hard inside of me.

Twenty-Four
Capshaw

The first few weeks of living with Kensy flew by, and it should have been unsettling that we adjusted so quickly to each other, but instead, it felt natural and unforced. When Lia questioned me about my feelings for Kensy the other day, I wanted to tell her that she was wrong and deny it, but the words were bitter on my tongue, refusing to be spoken.

But how could I already be so in love with someone I didn't know that long? Sure, I'd technically known Kensy since she was a kid, but I definitely didn't feel these feelings until recently when she came back. And the part that bothered me the most was that I didn't know if she felt the same way. We both knew that we had feelings for each other and technically were dating, but neither of us had bothered to say the L word yet.

It was Friday, and I was ending my 48-hour shift soon, which meant that I would have the entire weekend free with Kensy. I hadn't asked if she had any plans yet since we always seemed to hang out together without making any. But then again, she had been hanging out with Lia and Bella more these days, so I didn't want to assume. I pulled my phone out of my pocket and sent her a quick text message to see.

Me: Hey, beautiful. Do you have any plans this weekend?

It was already after six, so I knew her shift was over at Surf 'N Shack, and she would be home by now. It used to feel weird to call it "home" when referring to it being hers, but now it just felt like she belonged there. With me. In my arms. Or with me between her legs, which was where I spent a lot of my time lately.

Kensy: Lia and Bella are coming to get me soon. They're taking me out for a few drinks.

Me: Sounds fun.

Kensy: Unfortunately, I don't think I'm going to be much fun tonight. I told them to go without me, but they insisted I join them. I know they're just trying to cheer me up, but I'd rather stay home and be by myself.

I frowned at my phone, wondering what was wrong until it suddenly clicked. Kensy had mentioned to me recently that her dad's birthday was coming up, and she wasn't sure how she would handle it since it would be the first year they didn't celebrate.

Me: If you don't want to go, you shouldn't. I'll be home in an hour or so, and we can do something together instead if you want.

Me: And I don't mean sex—just in case that's what you were thinking. I meant something that will make you feel better. I know nothing can take away the pain of losing your dad, but we can still celebrate his birthday if you'd like.

Kensy: Thank you, that's very sweet of you, but I don't even know what I would do.

Me: What did you guys use to do for birthdays?

Kensy: For his birthday, we would always go fishing. We'd sit there all day until he caught something, then we'd go home, and he'd cook it for dinner. I would always make him his favorite cake, and then we'd stay up late watching action films.

Me: That sounds like a fun time. What was his favorite movie?

Kensy: *Gone In Sixty Seconds*. He also LOVED muscle cars.

Me: That movie is, hands down, one of the best movies. A true classic.

Kensy: I like it, but it wasn't my favorite.

Me: What's your favorite?

Kensy: Action or in general?

Me: Both.

Kensy: Action—I think probably *Gladiator*.

Me: I honestly didn't expect that to be your answer.

Kensy: Why not?

Me: I don't know, you just seem too young to have that be your favorite.

Kensy: My dad loved all things classic, which meant that we watched a lot of older movies. Heck, there was a time when we watched nothing but black-and-white movies for a few months.

Me: That sounds fun, though. So what's your favorite movie of all time?

Kensy: I love movies, so this is a hard question. It's like a mom trying to pick her favorite child! I mean, not my mom, but I'm sure normal moms who actually love their children.

Kensy didn't talk about her mother often, but I knew she still had deep-seated feelings toward her for abandoning her and her father when Kensy was little.

Kensy: I think my favorite movie of all time is *Pretty Woman*.

Me: You continue to surprise me. What makes that one your favorite out of all of them?

Kensy: It's simple—she's on her own with no one to help her, yet she finds a way to survive while also finding true love. She doesn't back down or give up. She holds her head high and does what she needs to create a better life for herself.

Me: Wow, it's quite impressive when you put it that way. Just like you are, Kensy.

Kensy: Thank you (smiley face emoji)

Kensy: Lia and Bella just got here, so I better let you go. See you tonight when I get home?

Me: You can count on it. Call me if you need a ride home or anything.

Kensy: Will do. Bye!

While I hated that I wouldn't get to see her when I got home, I knew that there was something else that needed my attention anyway. Tomorrow was her dad's birthday, and I was going to celebrate it with her and pray that I didn't royally fuck this up.

Twenty-Five

Kensy

"No more shots," I whined, pushing the shot glass away from me.

"Come on, don't be a baby." Lia narrowed her eyes and held it up.

"You know that getting me drunk isn't going to make me forget about tomorrow, right? It'll just ensure that I wake up with a hangover and feel like shit on top of being sad all day."

"I'm not trying to get you drunk," Lia countered. "You've only had one shot, and our tacos should be out any minute. I even asked for two sides of guacamole for you."

I rubbed my lips together, took the shot from her, and threw it back. Bella pounded her hands on the table and shook her head after she and Lia finished theirs. A few minutes later, our food arrived and I dove in. I was starving, and it was a known fact that guacamole couldn't be within a five-foot radius of me without me eating it.

"So, what's the plan for tomorrow?" Lia asked, shoving a chip into her mouth while Bella scraped some of the cheese off the top of her salad.

"What? I can't eat *and* drink my calories tonight—it has to be one or the other. I've had two shots which means some of this cheese has to go before it decides to take up residence on my ass," Bella sighed as Lia gave her a disapproving look.

"Hey, have you heard anything from Prestige?" I asked, hoping to take the attention off of tomorrow so we could enjoy dinner without me bursting into tears.

"I haven't yet, but thank you again for doing the photos for me. They came out GORGEOUS!"

"Not a problem, it was fun. I kinda wish I knew more women who wanted to do boudoir because, surprisingly, I enjoyed doing that more than I do the family sessions."

"I can talk to some of my friends and see if any of them would be interested," Bella offered, tossing more cheese to the side of her plate before Lia reached over, grabbed it, and shoved it into her mouth.

"What?" Lia laughed with her mouth full. "You don't want it to go to your hips, but I'm hoping it will go straight to my ass. Jerome is an ass guy."

"Who is Jerome?" I questioned before taking a bite out of my taco.

"Some new guy she met online," Bella answered with a shake of her head. "You know, you don't have to swipe right on *every* guy on that app."

"I don't. Just those with lots of tattoos and look like they can show me a good time. And spoiler alert—he's definitely a good time!"

"Lia!" I covered my mouth to keep from spitting out my food as I laughed. "Can you keep it in your pants for one second?"

"She can't. It's physically impossible—I've checked. And what's worse is that we'll be living together soon, and she's going to be the roommate that always has a sock on her doorknob, and I'll have to question where it's been before she put it there." Bella shuddered as Lia playfully elbowed her.

"You'll be just fine," Lia assured her. "Plus, we can create a system so we know who is getting some."

"Trust me—you'll be the only one in that system. I can't remember the last time I got laid, so I doubt that's going to be an issue. Are you sure you don't want to move in with us, Kensy? It's a three-bedroom house with two bathrooms. We can share a bathroom and let the sex fiend have the other one."

I laughed and shook my head. Had they asked me a few weeks ago, I might have considered, but now that things were going so well with Jack, I couldn't imagine living anywhere else. It felt right to be there, and things between us were always easy.

"How are *you* not getting any? You're freaking gorgeous and one of the nicest people I've ever met," I said to Bella.

"Aww, thank you. That's very sweet of you. But I don't date a lot because I'm usually busy with my modeling schedule, or the guys I meet think that because I'm a model, I'm an easy lay. I want someone who doesn't give a rat's ass about what I do or what I look like naked. I just want to meet someone who's genuinely nice and sincere and…."

Her sentence trailed off as she watched someone across the room. I turned around, my curiosity too high not to, and spotted Jones sitting in a booth with some of the guys from the firehouse. Jack wasn't with them, but they were all in regular clothes, which meant that they were off shift and Jack was probably at home—where I suddenly wanted to be.

"Who are you checking out?" Lia asked, beating me to it.

"No one." Bella's cheeks blushed the prettiest shade of pink as she looked down and poked at her salad with her fork.

"You're such a terrible liar. Just tell me who it is, and I'll have my brother help set you up."

"NO!" Bella shrieked, drawing the attention of those around us.

I carefully glanced over my shoulder and saw the guys looking at us, Jones's eyes suddenly lit up when he spotted us.

"Is it Jones?" I asked quietly, leaning across the table so Bella could hear me.

"No, it's nothing. I just spotted someone I recognized, and now everyone's making a big deal out of it."

I could see the anxiety and panic rolling off of her in waves.

"Speaking of seeing someone you recognize, guess who I ran into the other day at Surf 'N Shack?" I said to Lia, relieved at the way Bella's shoulders relaxed with the shift in conversation.

"Who?"

"Cole Turnsky."

"What? Since when is he back in town?" Her eyes widened before they narrowed with anger.

"Relax," I laughed, taking a sip of my water. "He's not back, just visiting his family and then heading back to Massachusetts."

"Good, he knows better than to stay here," Lia mumbled before taking a bite.

"Why? What did he do?" Bella asked.

I focused on finishing my food while Lia went into dramatic detail about Cole and how he copied her book report in seventh grade and got her sent to the principal's office. They had been enemies from that day on.

"He didn't even read the book! He watched the movie instead and then realized at the last minute that it wasn't the same and the teacher was going to catch on. So when I wasn't looking, he stole my book report and copied it without even asking. It was word for word—how stupid did he have to be to think that was going to work?!"

"It was such a long time ago. You've gotta move on and let it go," I said with a laugh, my stomach now painfully full after scarfing down three tacos and two bowls of guacamole.

"I can't," Lia huffed out. "He harassed me every day after that. Pulled my ponytail whenever he'd walk past me and tackled me during PE when it was *clearly* flag football and tackling wasn't allowed. I swear, he had it in for me."

"Maybe he liked you?" Bella offered with a shrug.

"Ha! I seriously doubt it. He was *the worst.*"

"Oh, come on, I wasn't *that* bad," a deep voice said before someone got up from the booth behind us and stood at our table.

I covered my mouth as I stared in disbelief. What were the odds that Cole would be here tonight—let alone sitting at the table right behind us?

"You were," Lia said sharply, not bothering to pretend that we hadn't just been talking about him.

His tall frame towered over us as piercing gray eyes

narrowed at Lia. He looked the same as he did back then, only his body went from scrawny preteen to a muscular and defined adult who knew how to rock a polo and cargo shorts like he belonged on the cover of a magazine.

"We'll have to agree to disagree," he said smoothly. "Unless you'll allow me to take you out to dinner so I can prove that I'm not as terrible as you believe I am."

"Over my dead body," Lia snarled, her eyes turning that icy blue color they get when she's mad.

"I mean, it's not the ideal way to do it," he joked, smiling and showcasing perfectly straight white teeth. "I usually rather my dates are alive and well."

"I'm not going on a date with you. Better get that idea out of your head and quick."

"I could focus on some of the other thoughts I have of you instead," he smirked.

"Do you see what I mean?" Lia exclaimed, holding her hands in front of her as she looked between Bella and me.

"I think he's charming," Bella said, gazing up at him as if he was the perfect man. "You should totally go to dinner with him, Lia. Maybe you'll learn something that will change your opinion about him."

"Ha! Not a chance in hell. He's only here for a short while, and then he'll be on his merry way back home. I can handle waiting it out until Beaumont Creek is free of him again."

He rubbed his lips together and looked at me.

"Hey, Kensy. Nice seeing you again."

"Hi," I offered a small wave and looked away. I felt bad for talking about him, to begin with, but I was just trying to help take the pressure off of Bella since she wasn't ready for us to know about her secret crush yet.

"I'm not heading back to Massachusetts," he confirmed, looking from me back to Lia. "I'm in town to look at a few houses. I plan to move back in a few months."

"Why?" Lia asked, her voice thick with suspicion.

"For work." He shrugged and said nothing else.

"Work?" She arched an eyebrow and continued to glare at him.

"Yeah, there's a program here that I recently got accepted to. But there's no need to get into that. I'll let you ladies enjoy your dinner. It was nice to see you again. I hope we can catch up later." He reached into his pocket, pulled out a business card, and set it down on the table in front of Lia.

After he was gone, I let out a heavy sigh and looked at Lia.

"Are you going to call him?" I asked as she held the card in front of her and read it.

"Not a chance in hell." She ripped it in half and tossed it into the bowl of salsa sitting in front of her.

Tonight turned out to be rather entertaining, though I still couldn't wait to go home and see Jack.

Twenty-Six
Capshaw

By the time Kensy got home last night, she had looked exhausted and smelled like tequila, so we cuddled for a bit until she fell asleep on the couch, and I carried her to bed. This morning I felt bad for waking her up early—especially if she had a hangover—but in order for my plan to work, we had to get the day started.

"Good morning," I whispered as I kissed her neck, smiling when she moaned softly and leaned into me. "It's time to get up, sleepy head."

She mumbled something into her pillow, but I couldn't make out what the words were. Though it sounded kind of like—wake me and die.

"Come on, baby, we gotta get going," I coaxed.

She rolled over onto her back and spread her legs, letting her head fall to the side as she went back to sleep.

"Kensy?" I laughed when she spread them even further.

"Go for it; I promise I'm into it."

I sat back on my heels and folded my arms.

"I'm not going to have sex with you while you're asleep, Kensy."

"Na," she whispered, eyes still closed. "I'm good. Awake. Ready. Set. Go."

The last word merged into a yawn.

"Ready, set, go? This isn't a race, you know?"

"It's okay if you finish first. I won't even be mad. Just stop talking and do it already."

"While that sounds *super* appealing, sex isn't on the agenda this morning. Now get up before I make you," I warned, my fingers trailing over the skin exposed beneath her t-shirt that rode up while she was sleeping.

"No sex?"

"No. Not right now. But we gotta get moving."

She rolled over onto her stomach and snuggled back into the pillow, so I smacked her ass and laughed when her head sprung off the bed.

"Jesus, Jack!" she yelped.

"I've been playing nice all morning. Now it's time to show you my other side if you don't get your ass up."

"The ass you just slapped?"

"The same ass that I'm going to drive my cock into in a few minutes if you don't stop talking back to me. Now let's go. I have a full day planned for us, and we're going to miss it if we don't get going."

"Fine," she mumbled and rolled out of bed.

I went to the master bathroom and turned on the shower for her so it could heat up before she got in. I'd already cleaned up and packed the stuff we needed while she slept, mainly because I knew that showering with Kensy would make us even later because we'd spend all morning fucking like we always did when I had a day off.

While she was getting ready, I packed the last few things in my truck and waited for her in the living room. I knew she had no idea what I had planned, but I loved that she wasn't fighting me on it. Trying to replicate what she always did with her dad was a huge risk, but it was better than sitting around the house all day, letting her cry. If she was going to do that, I wanted it to be while she was still celebrating him and not feeling like that part of her life was now over too.

Once we were on the road, I stopped for breakfast and then headed to my favorite fishing spot. I knew that Kensy might have an idea where we were going once I turned off and headed down a dirt road. The locals frequented this lake for as long as I could remember, and it was one of our best-kept secrets that the tourists never found out about. I noticed her shifting in her seat and glanced over to find tears in her eyes. I didn't say anything but reached over and held her hand as she cried.

I went past the spots that were already taken and headed to the end of the road, hoping that no one else was already there. Thankfully it was clear, so I parked, got out, and went around to open the door for her.

"You didn't have to do this, Jack," she said, accepting the hand I offered her as she climbed down.

"I know, I wanted to. It's John's birthday, and we're going to celebrate him. But if it becomes too much or you want to leave, just say the word. Okay?"

"Should I use okra again?" she teased, wiping the tears away with the palms of her hands.

"Totally up to you," I laughed and started unpacking the truck.

I'd brought plenty of food and water since I didn't know how long we would be out here but left the ice chest in the truck until we needed it. Kensy decided to wear a sundress which made me feel better about my decision to bring the camping chairs so she didn't have to sit on the ground and have something bite her ass since I'd noticed she was also wearing a thong underneath it. I was convinced she was trying to kill me until I reminded myself she had no idea what I had planned for today.

Kensy jumped in, helped me set up the rods, and got them situated while I took care of the bait. I knew she'd done this a million times with her dad, but I was still impressed with her skills as she took control and got everything ready.

I wasn't sure if there was anything to say or do before we cast our lines in the water, but I wanted to ensure that we honored John as much as possible.

"To John," I said, holding my rod in the air while making sure the light breeze didn't blow my hook into Kensy's face as she held hers. "Happy birthday. We hope you're up in heaven, guiding us to where the fish are so we can make you proud today."

I heard Kensy sniffle as the tears started rolling down her face again.

"Happy birthday, dad. I love and miss you so much."

There were plenty of things that I did in my everyday life

that didn't bother me because I had trained myself to put up a shield of armor and keep my emotions at bay. Running into burning buildings. Saving children and cats from fires. Having to be there when someone's loved one didn't make it and watching them grieve as officers broke the news. All of that was hard, but I could handle it. The one thing that I couldn't take was seeing Kensy cry.

I dropped my rod to the ground and pulled hers away from her before wrapping her in my arms and holding her against my chest as she broke down and cried. I knew that the past few months had been hard on her, but she never showed it, and now I wondered just how much she had been hiding from everyone, pretending to be okay.

"Shhh, it's okay," I whispered. "Let it out, Kensy. I've got you."

"I miss him so much it hurts," she cried, her body trembling against mine.

"I can't begin to imagine, baby. I hate that I can't do anything to lessen some of that pain for you. I know he was a good man, and you don't deserve to have lost him."

"He was my only family. When my mom left, my dad didn't even freak out. He just said, 'well, it's just you and me now, kid. Let's make this the best life we can.' And he did, Jack. He gave me a beautiful life. Taught me so many things and made sure that I was happy. And now he's gone, and I don't know who I am without him. I don't know how I'm supposed to live this life without the only person who's ever loved me."

She cried harder as the tears rolled down my face. I couldn't help it, she was breaking my heart, and I felt her pain as if it were my own.

I gently pulled her away from me so I could see her face, even though I wasn't sure she could see me through all of the tears clouding her eyes.

"He's not the only person, Kensy. Not by a long shot. I've been waiting for the right time to say this, but now I hate myself for not saying it sooner. I love you with everything I have. I'm head over heels, completely and madly in love with you. Please don't ever question whether you're loved because I will go to my grave trying to show you just how much you are. I know it's not the same love your dad gave you, but I love you so damn much, Kensy."

She desperately wiped at her face, trying to clear her tears before she reached up and wrapped her arms around my neck.

"I love you too, Jack. I have for a while, but I've been so afraid to say it out loud."

"Why, baby?"

"Because other than my dad, the last person that I told I love you to was my mom. She didn't say it back. She just turned around, got into a cab, and left. She didn't care that I was crying. She didn't look back. She just went on with her life, not bothered by any of it. I haven't said it to anyone other than my dad since then."

"I'm so sorry, Kensy. You don't deserve any of that. But rest assured, I will always tell you how much I love you from here on, whether ten times a day or one hundred. I'll never get tired of making sure you feel it. You deserve to feel loved, and it's my mission to make sure that's happening."

We stayed there for a while, with me holding her, our hearts dancing to the same beat as if they were destined to be together all along.

Twenty-Seven
Kensy

We spent the first half of the day talking while we waited for anything to bite, but the rods went untouched as the fish went about their merry way, not at all impressed with the bait we used. It was a beautiful day out, not too hot, and thankfully, Jack had picked a spot under some thick trees that provided plenty of shade. I also loved that we were at the end of the road and that the brush was so thick on both sides that it kept anyone from entering our space. Every now and then, we heard the voices of others fishing nearby, but it was nice not having to share this area with anyone.

My mind was still spinning after hearing Jack say that he loved me. I knew that I loved him for a while now, but I wasn't willing to go first in saying it. I also wasn't lying when I said that my dad was the only person I've ever said I love you to after my mom didn't say it back. I didn't date much in high school, and even the few guys I was with in college never got to the "love" stage. They were nice and decent in bed, but there was never anything more than that, unlike what I felt with Jack. That was how I knew I'd fallen in love with him but was too scared to admit it.

By lunchtime, Jack pulled a blanket out of his truck and set up a beautiful picnic with all of my favorite foods—including a bag of Sour Patch Kids. We hung out on the blanket for a while, talking while I chewed their heads off and tossed their bodies back into the bag. I wasn't sure how long he was planning to stay out here, but I didn't want to tie up his entire day when he was just trying to do something nice for me.

"We can go whenever you want," I offered, looking up at the sky as clouds started rolling in. It was almost four, and we still hadn't caught a damn thing.

"Nope, we're not leaving until we catch something."

Jack looked rather comfortable sitting in the camping chair with his legs spread out in front of him, ankles crossed.

"We're more likely to catch a cold from that storm rolling in than a fish," I teased, nodding to the dark clouds.

"Eh, I'm not afraid of the rain. But if you're cold, I think I have a hoodie in the truck you can borrow. Or you can come sit with me, and I'll warm you up."

I moved my eyes back and forth as I pretended to consider the options, then I got up, walked over to where he was sitting, and waited for him to get comfortable before I sat down. The chair was surprisingly big enough to fit both of us as I sat on his lap with my legs resting across his. He pulled me into his chest and kept one arm around my waist while his other hand laid on my thighs, the warmth of it seeping through the thin fabric of my dress.

"You know you're killing me in this dress, right?" he asked, his voice thick.

"You don't like it?" I teased, lifting the bottom playfully before his hand clasped down to stop me.

"You're playing with fire," he warned.

I took a deep breath and locked eyes with him as I let it out.

"Then I guess it's a good thing you're a firefighter, huh?"

He pulled his lower lip between his teeth, making me want to lean in and bite it. I licked my lips, his eyes watching my every move.

"Fuck, Kensy," he growled, his fingers digging into my sides as if he was trying to restrain himself.

"What's wrong, Jack?" I played innocent, batting my eyes.

"You make this so hard."

"What? This?" I asked, reaching my hand in between my legs to touch his cock that was growing beneath my ass.

He pinched his eyes shut and stilled.

"Well, that's not a problem. I know exactly how to take care of that."

He opened his eyes and arched an eyebrow as I climbed off his lap.

"What are you doing?" he asked as I bent in front of him, my dress falling forward and allowing him a glimpse of the lacy black bra I had on while my hands reached for his zipper and pulled it down.

"Problem-solving." I shrugged and reached in, struggling to free him from his boxer briefs as I pulled him out of the opening in his pants.

"Someone could catch us," he warned.

"Then we better be quiet."

"That means no screaming as you come."

"I'll do my best," I agreed. "Do you have a condom?"

"In my wallet, but I have to stand up to get it."

I stepped back to give him some room and admired his cock as it jutted out, my body desperate to feel him inside of me.

He quickly got it out of his wallet and rolled it onto his dick in record-breaking time. Okay, so I don't know if it was really record-breaking, but we'll just say that my vagina was quite impressed with his speed and willingness to move this party along.

He sat down and gripped the arms of the chair as I backed up to him and sat down, pulling my dress up and thong to the side. I would have taken it off, but one thing I learned about Jack early on was that he loved fucking me with my panties on.

His fingers gripped my hips and helped guide me onto his cock, a sharp hiss coming out of his mouth once I was situated and sunk down on him. No matter how many times we did it, I never got over how fucking incredible it felt to have him deep inside me, filling every single bit of space there was.

I rocked my hips back and forth, finding a rhythm we both liked while his hands caressed my breasts. No one was around, so I didn't mind when he pulled the fabric of my dress down and then released them over the cups of my bra so he could pinch my nipples as I rode him harder.

I was fucking him like my life depended on it, grinding against him as my orgasm started to build. He kept playing with my nipples until he felt my thighs squeeze together, knowing I was getting close. I felt his fingers as they dipped into my panties and began rubbing my clit, nearly sending me over the edge as my body blazed on fire.

I was about to close my eyes and let myself go when I spotted one of the rods moving. I thought it must have been the breeze until I saw a hard jerk, then another.

"Fish," I cried out, then bit down on my lip as he made another circle around my clit. "Fuuuckkk," I cried out. "Fish. Fish. Fish."

"Yeah, baby. That's it. Come for me."

"No, fish," I panted, watching the rod jerk harder. I was close—so close—to coming, but I also didn't want to miss out on catching something today.

"FISH!" I screamed as he rubbed harder, my pussy spasming around him as the orgasm consumed me.

We were both panting, my back resting against his chest as we tried to catch our breath.

"That was amazing," he said, tucking a strand of hair behind my ear before kissing my cheek.

"There was a fish," I replied, pointing to the line that was now still in the water.

"Oh, shit!"

He started to push me off of him, then realized what he was doing and gently lifted and placed me in the seat as he got up. He pulled the condom off, wrapped it in one of the paper towels from lunch, then tossed it in the trash bag while he rushed to tuck himself back in.

I got up and fixed my dress, making sure my boobs were in the right place and that my thong wasn't stuck up my ass anymore.

I followed him over to the rod as he handed it to me and nodded.

"Reel it in, see if it's still on the line," he said.

Nervously I took it from him and started to reel it in, worried that the fish wasn't there since there wasn't any resistance. We were both silent, holding our breath until the end of the line suddenly surfaced above the water, and on the hook was the most beautiful catfish I had ever seen.

Twenty-Eight
Jack

Spending the day celebrating Kensy's dad's birthday with her was more rewarding than I would have ever imagined. Once we caught one fish, we called it a day and got home right before the storm started. The dark clouds that had been looming above us at the lake were gracious enough to allow us to pack up and get on the road before the downpour started.

I worked on frying the catfish since I knew a thing or two about that from growing up working at The Surf 'N Shack, while Kensy made the most delicious german chocolate cake I'd ever tasted. What was even better was how sweet it tasted between her thighs as I spread it across her lips and teased her as I licked it off. The taste of Kensy on my tongue was better than the cake I ate from between her folds after sliding it inside with my finger. One thing that we always enjoyed was bringing food into our foreplay.

We were exhausted from a long day at the lake, followed by an evening of making love, and called it an early night for once. The rest of the weekend was relaxing, and by Monday night, I was dreading going on shift again and being away from her.

When I walked into the firehouse, the smell of burnt rubber greeted me, assaulting my nostrils as I pinched my nose to keep it from permeating.

"What the fuck is that smell?" I asked Nate as I set my duffle bag down on the bench and opened my locker.

"Jones made breakfast."

"Do I even want to ask?"
Nate shook his head.

"But it's your turn to teach him to cook, so you're officially on duty." He slapped a hand on my shoulder as he walked off, chuckling on the way.

I changed into my turnout gear and then followed the stench to the kitchen, where Jones was standing next to something that was burnt black and still had flames flickering along the top. I grabbed the fire extinguisher from the wall and put it out as he stepped back and covered his face with his hands.

We didn't speak as I put it back and stood next to him, staring at the disaster in the pan.

"Do I want to ask?"

"Cinnamon rolls."

I arched an eyebrow and turned to him.

"How the hell did you catch cinnamon rolls on fire? What was in the recipe? Bourbon?"

"There wasn't a recipe," he said, shaking his head and rubbing a hand along his neck.

"No recipe? What did you use?"

He turned his head to look at me, and his face reddened with embarrassment.

"I bought the ones that come in the can."

"Okay…."

I waited for him to continue as I bit the inside of my cheek to keep from laughing.

"What happened?"

"I don't know. I put them in the pan, loaded them into the oven, and then a few minutes later, I heard a loud pop—like something exploded. Then I came in here to check them, and when I opened the oven, they were on fire. I pulled the pan out and set it on the stove, but the flames just got higher. That's when you came in."

I rubbed my lips with my finger, trying to keep it together. Jones was one of the sweetest kids I knew, but he couldn't cook to save his life.

"Umm, Jones?"

"Yeah?"

"Did you take the cinnamon rolls out of the container before you put them in the oven?"

He reached up and covered his face with his hands.

"No."

I nodded and was about to finally laugh when I heard an alarm sound from the other room. Jones looked at me, confusion on his face.

"It's the Safe Haven Baby Box," I explained, rushing to the box as a few of the other guys headed in the same direction as Jones followed me.

By the time I reached it, the second alarm was going on,

notifying us that a baby had been placed inside. Nate was first to get to the box and quickly pulled the bassinet out so he could secure the baby.

My heart was racing, not knowing what to do as this was the first time we'd ever had anyone utilize the box. I'd been through plenty of training courses about the box, but now that it was happening, it felt like I had forgotten everything I knew.

"Is it okay?" I asked, leaning forward to see that baby in Nate's arms.

"Seems like it so far, but we'll need to take the baby to the hospital for evaluation. They'll handle things from there."

We all stood there for a few minutes, watching the baby as if it was going to suddenly need us to jump into action and rescue it.

"I'll go ahead and make the call to let them know we're coming," Nate said.

"Hey, Captain, there's an envelope that must've been tucked under the baby," Rodriguez said, holding it up. "It's umm…."

"It's what?" Nate asked.

Rodriguez sucked in a deep breath and then looked me dead in the eye.

"It's addressed to Capshaw."

What. The. Fuck.

Twenty-Nine
Capshaw

Capshaw,

I know you are probably confused—hell, I was too, when I found myself staring down at a positive pregnancy test nine months ago. I refused to believe that I—of all people—could be pregnant. I waited a few weeks and took another test, only to find out it was also positive. By the time I saw a doctor, I was already ten weeks pregnant and had moved to New York City.

You're also probably wondering why I didn't reach out and tell you that we had created a baby together. But if you remember that night like I do, we both agreed that it would be just one time and we would never see each other again.

A lot has changed for me since that night, and unfortunately, not for the better. When I was six months pregnant, I lost my job. Being that far along made it difficult to find something else, as no one wanted to hire someone that would be taking extended leave soon. Without a job, I wasn't able to pay my rent and ended up getting evicted when I was eight months pregnant. I had been struggling to make ends meet for a while, but it finally caught up to me, and I lost the only safe place I had.

I knew I had no other option but to find you and see if you could help. I hitchhiked my way back to Beaumont Creek a week ago and went into labor before I got to you. I know this isn't something you were expecting, and I'm sorry.

I've done a lot of things wrong and made plenty of poor choices along the way, but the one thing that I know I'm finally doing right is giving our daughter a chance to have a life I can't give her. I hope that you'll take one look at her and feel the connection like I did when they placed her in my arms.

She's your baby, Capshaw. Please don't abandon her or turn her away because you don't believe me. Get a paternity test, and confirm that she's yours if you need that peace of mind, but please do not give her up.

Leaving her in the Safe Haven Baby Box was one of the hardest things I've ever had to do. I love her more than anyone will ever know. I know that you don't owe me a single thing, but please tell her how much I love her. When she's old enough to start asking about me, please tell her that I did what I could to save her when I couldn't save myself. That's all I ask.

I've made a hard decision by leaving her, but I know that it comes with consequences. I won't come back later demanding anything from you or asking to see her. I understand that it's not fair to either of you and it's a burden I'll have to bear.

You have my word that she's yours. I'm including as much information about me as possible so that if she asks about me someday, you can decide whether to try to find me or not. If you feel that she deserves to know me, I hope that you'll make an effort to do that for her.

I named her Brayleigh because it means "ray of hope," and that's what she was for me.

Please love and take care of my baby for me. That's all that I ask.

Always,

Zoe

Thirty
Kensy

"Can I get you anything else?" I asked, hoping the guy in front of me would stop flirting with me so I could sneak to the back and check my phone that kept vibrating in my pocket.

He said something about my number, so I plastered on a phony smile and handed him a plastic one with a holder for his table.

"Have a good day," I said as he rolled his eyes and stormed off.

There wasn't anyone in line for the first time in over an hour, so I pulled my phone out and checked to see who was calling and why. Only it wasn't a phone call but several messages from Jack.

Jack: Hey, what time do you get off today?

Jack: I need to talk to you. Do you want to do dinner?

Jack: Sorry, I don't think I can do dinner. Something has come up.

Jack: I didn't mean to worry you, sorry. Call me when you can.

Jack: I'm heading to the hospital and might be there for a while. Everything is fine. I'll call you soon.

I kept staring at the messages, wondering what was going on when another rush of customers came in. Jack's dad had been suffering from some pain after working the register the past few days, so I assured him I would man it today so he could rest in his office and try to reduce the swelling. Lia was supposed to come in later to take over, but that was still a few hours away.

I hated that Jack sounded like something was wrong and I couldn't talk to him to find out what it was. Not only that—why was he at the hospital? My mind was racing, and I found it was getting harder to focus on what people were ordering without screwing them up. Finally, Natalie started her shift and took over the register while I offered to clear tables and run orders. I needed to be busy and active without having to focus mentally on anything right now.

When Lia came in, she didn't say anything about Jack or give me any hints as to what was going on, so I didn't bother to ask. I knew that sometimes Jack was super private with what he shared with his family compared to what he shared with me, and I didn't want him to feel like he couldn't talk to me anymore.

Finally, my shift was over and as I was clocking out, I felt my phone vibrate again.

Jack: I'll be home in an hour. Will you be there?

Me: Yes. Is everything okay? I've been worried about you all day but didn't get any breaks to call you.

Jack: Everything is okay, but I have something we need to discuss when I get there.

Me: I'm getting worried, Jack.

Jack: It'll be okay. I promise.

Thirty-One
Capshaw

Why did I promise Kensy that everything would be okay? It wasn't—not by a long shot. Not only did Zoe leave me the letter explaining why she was leaving her daughter with me, but she'd also included the legal paperwork granting me full custody of Brayleigh that she had drawn up right before she lost her apartment. According to a note inside, she spent the last bit she had in her savings to get it done because she already knew at that point that she wouldn't be able to care for her and didn't want me to have a hard time taking custody of *my daughter*.

It still sounded weird to hear that word coming out of my mouth. Yesterday I was enjoying my day at home, thinking dirty thoughts about Kensy and what I was going to do to her when she got home from work, and today I was walking aimlessly down the diaper aisle while Nate told me about what brand he liked best.

How the fuck did I get here?

"You're going to want the super absorbent ones," he said, tossing a pack into the shopping cart that was already filled to the top with supplies. "Don't worry, Abby will be here soon to help pick out clothes."

"That's the least of my concerns right now," I mumbled as I bounced my daughter gently, making sure she could still breathe as her face pressed against my chest in the baby carrier Nate had loaned me.

"It's a lot, I get it." He stopped and turned toward me, genuine sympathy in his eyes. "With Penny, I had nine months to get used to the idea of being a dad. Hell, even longer than that since we were purposely trying to get Abby pregnant when we started fooling around. This was just dropped on you, and now you have to change your whole life in a heartbeat. You're an instant dad with no warning that it was coming."

"I'm going to fuck this up," I said quietly, placing my hand over her ear so she didn't hear me. "I have no idea how to care for a baby, Nate. No fucking idea. This is going to be worse than anything Jones has ever done in the kitchen."

"Hey, I heard that." Jones came around the corner holding a few cans of formula, holding them up.

"Sorry. I'm just stressed."

"It's okay; you don't have to apologize. It's not a secret that I don't know how to cook. But one thing that I do know is babies. The benefit of constantly moving from foster home to foster home—there were always lots of other kids, and most of them were babies."

"*You* know about babies?" I asked Jones in disbelief.

"That I do. And since you always help me, I shall help in return. Now, for formula—I grabbed these two, but you're welcome to check out the rest. Since you don't know if she has a sensitive stomach, I picked the gentle formula. The last thing you want is a super gassy baby that gets fussy. When is her first pediatric appointment?"

"Umm," I closed my eyes and tried to think. "The hospital

said that she's three days old, according to their records of when Zoe came in and gave birth. I think they set one up for tomorrow. Honestly, it's all been a blur, and I can't remember."

Nate pulled out his phone, pressed some buttons, then held it to his ear.

"Hey, Sabrina, it's Nate. Can you confirm an appointment that was scheduled today? It's for Jack Capshaw's newborn daughter, Brayleigh Capshaw."

My stomach turned hearing those words together. I had no idea how I was going to explain all of this to Kensy tonight.

"Perfect. Can you make sure that the appointment is with Jane?" Nate continued to scan the aisle we were on, adding a few random things to my cart while he waited. "Wonderful. Thank you for your help, Sabrina. He'll see Jane tomorrow."

"Tomorrow," I confirmed once he hung up. "I'm seeing a girl I slept with about a baby I didn't even know I had with another girl I slept with shortly after her."

"You're fine; let's finish grabbing the rest of what you need." Nate led the way while Jones pushed another cart that they began adding stuff to.

"There's more? What else could I possibly need?"

Nate and Jones stopped, looked at each other, then started laughing. I followed along, completely lost and already in over my head.

By the time we were done, all 3 of our trucks were packed full of baby furniture and bags of baby stuff they assured me I needed. What I really wanted to know was who was going to move in with me and teach me how to use all of it.

I asked them to give me a few minutes to talk to Kensy before they rushed in with everything and started helping me set up. I had been given the next few days off shift while I got situated while Nate and Jones were technically on duty if a call came in.

Kensy had texted me as we were checking out and asked if I wanted her to start dinner. I told her no, that I would order takeout when I got home but left out the part about how I was too nauseous to eat anything at this point. I would make sure she ate, but I couldn't even guarantee that she would stick around long enough to eat once she found out that I now had a baby.

I pulled into the driveway slowly, making sure I didn't hit the brakes too hard as I watched Brayleigh sleep in her car seat. I was hopeful that maybe this whole baby thing would be easier than I thought, given that she'd been sleeping the majority of the time since I had her.

I got out and tried to remember everything Nate showed me when we installed the car seat, even though I technically knew from being a firefighter. I could teach parents how to install a car seat in my sleep, but I felt completely clueless now that it was my baby. I unfastened the straps and gently pulled her out, cradling her against my chest before grabbing the diaper bag we set up in the parking lot and heading inside.

The door swung open as Kensy greeted me on the other side, a look of concern quickly replaced by confusion.

"Hey," I said cautiously, bouncing Brayleigh as she started to fuss. I stepped inside and closed the door behind me as Kensy kept watching us, unsure of what was happening.

"Hi." Her voice was higher than normal and guarded. "Is everything okay?"

I set the diaper bag down and nodded as I took a deep breath.

"Umm, this is Brayleigh."

"Brayleigh?"

"My daughter."

"Your *what*?"

"That's exactly what I said a few hours ago."

Her eyes widened so much that they looked like they might pop out of her head.

"I'm sorry—what?"

"She was left in the Safe Haven Baby Box at the fire station earlier with a note from a woman I slept with nine months ago. There are legal documents confirming that I am the sole guardian of her, but I requested a paternity test while I was at the hospital earlier."

Kensy blinked slowly a few times and looked from me to the baby, who was now waking up on my chest.

"How old is she?"

"Three days old."

"Three days?"

I nodded, giving her the time she needed to process this. It was huge, and I hadn't been able to give her a heads-up before I got here.

She walked over to the couch and sat down, so I joined her.

"I don't understand," she muttered, looking at the baby in my arms again.

I turned her around now that she was fully awake and made sure to support her head.

"Honestly, I'm still trying to do the same," I admitted.

"You have a baby."

"It looks that way," I sighed. "Nate and Jones are on their way over soon to drop off the stuff they convinced me to buy at the store. I think Abby might be coming too. I honestly don't even know what's going on anymore."

"Have you told your family yet?" she asked, tilting her head to the side as what looked like a million thoughts ran through her mind.

"No, besides the guys, you're the first person I've told. They only know because they were there when everything happened. Nate and Jones went with me to the hospital to have her checked out, then took me to the store to get the stuff I needed."

"What if she's not yours? Will you give her up?"

Kensy's shoulders tightened as she thought about it.

"I don't know. I'm not making any rash decisions right now. I have paperwork granting me custody, and until I get the results back from the paternity test, I'm going to treat her as my daughter and step up to the plate to be the best father she could ever have."

Kensy smiled the first smile I'd seen since she found out the news a few minutes ago.

"I'm going to go start dinner. I'll make plenty to feed everyone since you'll have company soon. But Jack, if I can make one small recommendation?"

"Of course, anything."

"Call your family now and tell them. Your mother will be devastated if she finds outs from someone else. You know small towns and how they talk—get ahead of it now. Invite her and your dad and Lia over for dinner and to meet your daughter."

My heart felt like it was going to burst. I wasn't sure what to expect from Kensy, but feeling how supportive she was right now made me fall even more in love with her.

Thirty-Two
Kensy

I made what felt like 50 pounds of spaghetti and three loaves of garlic bread for dinner while Jack fed Brayleigh. His family joined us for dinner, and after everyone finished eating—and passing the baby around because they couldn't get enough of her—the guys all retreated to Jack's room to help assemble the crib.

I had offered to give up my space in his guest room so he could turn it into a nursery, but he assured me that he wanted to keep Brayleigh as close to him as possible until he got the hang of the whole *dad thing*. He also made sure that I knew that I was still invited to sleep in his bed like I had been doing and that this didn't change anything.

Lia and Bella were working on sorting through the laundry that had just come out of the dryer while I helped his mom fold and put stuff away in the dresser he bought for her. I had never seen so many pink and purple onesies in my life and giggled at how Jack's semi-masculine house was about to get a very girly makeover.

Abby had helped pick out the clothes, blankets, bedding, and towels for Brayleigh but didn't come with Nate to help set up since their daughter wasn't feeling well, and she didn't want to risk getting the new baby sick. I felt slightly jealous that she got to be there with him, shopping for his baby instead of me.

But then I realized I was being ridiculous and pushed those insecurities out of my head because I knew there was plenty of other stuff to worry about.

"I think we're running out of room," I commented, pushing another onesie into the drawer and closing it. "I think we might need another dresser, or we might have to start hanging some of this up."

"I can see if Capshaw has room in his closet," Lia offered as she came into the guest room and handed her mom another pile of clothes.

They had set the dresser up in there because there wasn't room in his bedroom for it, and the guest room was spacious enough to fit it. It didn't bother me that I would technically be sharing my space with the baby because it wasn't my house, and I was just a temporary guest—though we never talked about how temporary it would be.

It wasn't like Jack knew he was having a baby and had time to set up for her. All of this came crashing down on him, and he was forced to figure out how to make things work without time to think them through. We all assured him that it would be fine to get them started and that we could move stuff around and make changes if needed.

"If you don't mind? I've stuffed as much as I can in here, but between onesies, shirts, pants, socks, and sweaters, I think I'm finally out of room." I looked at the dresser and wondered whether he should have gotten a bigger one. It wasn't too wide and had four drawers that looked deep until I started filling them.

A few minutes later, Jack came in and wrapped his arms around my waist as he planted a kiss on my cheek. At first I was nervous about his mom seeing us together like this, but then she smirked and kept working on the pile Lia brought in, so I knew she already knew.

"Lia said that you ran out of room for Brayleigh's stuff in here," he said, still holding on to me.

"Yeah, I've fit as much as I can in it, but it's crammed full, and I worry that if I put anything else in it, you won't be able to open it."

"I should have gotten the one with double the number of drawers. I thought for sure this would work—she's a tiny baby, how much could she possibly need?"

"A lot," his mom laughed, setting down the clothes in her hands and smiling at us. "Babies need a lot, Capshaw. But it's okay. You'll make this work. You'll figure out a way just like you always do."

"I appreciate your faith in me, mom, but I hate to tell you that I have no flipping clue what I'm doing."

"No one does. That's part of the parenting experience. We all start out knowing nothing and learn as we go. Trust me, you'll be just fine." She got up and rubbed a hand along his face. "Now, if you'll excuse me, I'm going to go steal my granddaughter from your dad. I need more baby snuggles."

She walked out and left us alone, the first time we'd had since everyone arrived a few hours ago. I turned and faced him, his arms still wrapped around my waist.

"I think they like her," he teased, pressing his lips to mine.

"I think they *love* her," I corrected. "It's pretty hard not to; she's such a cutie."

"Are you okay with all of this?"

"It's a lot to take in," I admitted, starting to pull away until his arms locked tighter to hold me in place. "But we can take everything day by day and figure out what all of this looks like."

His brows pinched together but he still refused to let go.

"What do you mean? What do we need to figure out?"

"There's a lot that's changing and quick, Jack. You took me in and let me stay with you, but we never talked about how long that would be. You won't even let me pay you rent," I laughed nervously.

"Okay, so what's the problem with that? I like having you stay here, and I don't need your money, Kensy. I can afford the mortgage and utilities on my own. We agreed that I would buy the groceries and you would help cook. Nothing has changed between us or the agreements we've made."

"No, but there's another person involved now, and that person is going to need a lot from you, Jack. And as you can see, she's going to be an added expense," I said, breaking free from his arms and spreading my arms in front of me, showing him how much the baby's stuff had already taken over my room.

"I can afford the change, Kensy. I promise. You don't have to worry about getting kicked out or finding a new place to stay."

"But what about when she gets bigger and you want her to have her own space? You only have one guest room, Jack, and I don't think she will want to be cramped in this room with me."

"Then you move into my room, and she can have the guest room as her room."

"You don't get it," I said, frustrated, though I wasn't sure why. "I don't want to be in the way, especially when her needs should come first. It's that feeling of not knowing where I'm going or what I'm doing that makes me feel antsy. I know that you offered me to stay with you, but that was before all of this happened. I don't know that there's a place for me anymore, and that's okay. But I need to feel like I can put roots down somewhere, Jack, and that's what's making me feel anxious because I don't feel like I can easily do that here."

Jack crossed his arms over his chest and nodded his head while his full lips pursed together.

"Okay, fine."

My head snapped back, unsure of how to process his words. He didn't sound angry, but it was such a short response that I didn't know how to take it.

He pushed past me and stepped into the closet, grabbing a handful of my clothes from the closet and pulling them free. Then he walked out of the bedroom, hangers falling off some of the shirts as he went down the hallway and into his bedroom.

"What are you doing?" I asked, following him in and smiling nervously at Nate and Jones, who were finishing building the crib.

"I'm moving you into my bedroom. We'll store your clothes in the closet, and then I'll clear out a few drawers in my dresser for you to use."

"Jack," I sighed, rubbing my fingers against my temple. "You don't have to do this. I think you missed the point of what I was saying."

"No, Kensy, I think you're missing the point. I love you and want you to feel welcome in *our* house. We should have moved your stuff in here already, but we didn't, so I'm taking care of it now. That will free up the closet in the guest room, which we can set up as the nursery. Problem solved."

I stepped to the side as he walked past me and grabbed more clothes from my closet. He was a man on a mission, and I wasn't going to stand in his way.

Thirty-Three
Capshaw

Spoiler alert—I was wrong when I thought that Brayleigh would be an easy baby because she slept so much. Last night was rough, and no matter how hard I tried, I couldn't get her to stay asleep unless I held her. On top of that, she was up every few hours to eat and needed to be changed.

By morning, Kensy and I both looked like zombies as we gravitated toward the coffee machine. I had Brayleigh cuddled to my chest while Kensy started a pot of coffee for us, then we traded while I made breakfast and she fixed her a bottle.

We realized quickly last night that Brayleigh did better with Kensy feeding her, and while she was convinced that it was because her energy was calmer, I knew that it was because Kensy had soft, plush boobs and I didn't. If it were me— that's where I would want to be.

I was exhausted but knew we needed to eat before the day started. My parents had given Kensy the rest of the week off so she could help me get situated. Bella had stepped in to help cover her shifts, and I had to keep myself from laughing when Jones immediately volunteered to help on his days off this week, knowing that he would definitely catch something on fire if he were allowed anywhere near the kitchen. But I didn't step in and tell my parents no when they agreed to it, especially when I saw the way he was looking at Bella.

The bacon sizzled in the skillet, reminding me I needed to be more alert when grease splattered out and burned my arm. I pulled them out of the pan and set them on a paper towel to absorb the excess grease while I plated the rest of the food.

I walked into the living room to find her with Brayleigh over her shoulder, patting her back as she tried to get her to burp. We'd found that she was a difficult one, and neither of us had discovered the ideal position that worked best.

"Here, I can hold her while you eat," I offered, setting our plates on the coffee table and then taking the baby from her.

"Thank you for making breakfast. It smells delicious."

"Thank you for feeding Brayleigh. You had the harder job between the two of us," I teased, positioning her on my shoulder so I could try to eat with my other hand.

Kensy smiled and then took her plate, balancing it on the pillow on her lap. We ate quickly, knowing we still had to get ready before heading to Brayleigh's doctor's appointment. I asked Kensy if she wanted to go with me and she said sure, but I tried not to read too much into the lack of enthusiasm I thought I heard in her voice. It wasn't her baby, and it was unrealistic to assume that she would just jump on board with helping me raise her when this was literally sprung on her yesterday. Hell, I hadn't even had time to process all of this, let alone been able to ask her how she felt about it. For now, we were both just trying to go with the flow and prayed that the flow didn't lead us down a river where we would drown.

We finished our food, and Kensy took our dishes to the kitchen before jumping in the shower. Brayleigh was getting fussy, so I stood up and bounced her on my shoulder as I walked around the living room. I figured she was tired, but she kept pulling her legs under her and crying. I wasn't sure if maybe she was having growing pains, but whatever it was sure seemed to be hurting her.

I was just about to interrupt Kensy's shower to ask for help when she returned. Brayleigh had been screaming for a solid fifteen minutes, and nothing I did stopped it. I was about to lose my mind when suddenly the room was filled with a loud rumbling sound.

Kensy's eyes widened as my jaw dropped, both of us shocked by the loudest fart that just came out of this teeny tiny baby.

"Well, I guess that explains why she was so fuss—" I started but then stopped when I felt a warm wetness spread down my shirt.

I closed my eyes as Kensy burst into laughter.

"I don't want to know how bad it is, do I?"

"No," she giggled. "But you're definitely going to need a shower. So is she."

"Fuck."

She giggled harder and I felt my mood lighten.

"Alright, how do we do this?" I asked, holding my daughter's butt as she cuddled into me and started to fall asleep. Apparently being covered in shit didn't bother her one bit.

"Honestly? I think we should get both of you in the shower, rinse this off, and then I can clean her up and get her ready.

We can leave the wet clothes in there for now, and I'll toss them in the washer when we get back since we're already running late."

"Alright, you lead the way."

Kensy laughed as she went ahead of me, looking over her shoulder every few seconds to make sure I was coming. She turned the hot water on and then adjusted it to warm before I got in with Brayleigh. I kept her face out of the water but allowed it to rinse the poop off her clothes as Kensy took her onesie off and tossed it to the shower floor. The poop had shot up her back, a liquid mess that thankfully washed off fairly easily in the shower.

I held her to my chest while Kensy got the diaper off, then quickly washed her with some lavender baby wash that smelled delicious and calming, making sure to avoid getting her umbilical cord wet. Once Brayleigh was clean, Kensy wrapped her in a towel and took her to the living room to get her ready while I rushed my shower to make sure we got to her appointment on time. I didn't want to be late, but I also knew that Jane would appreciate me taking a few minutes to get the smell of poop off of my skin before we got there.

The morning already felt chaotic and stressful, but the waiting room of the doctor's office was even worse. Kids were crying and throwing fits as their parents tried their best to keep them calm. Kensy assured me that it wasn't that bad, but in my head, I envisioned this being what World War 3 might look like, and I was terrified.

"Brayleigh," a nurse called, holding a clipboard while she waited for us at the door that led back to the patient rooms.

I smiled as I got up and grabbed the car seat she was sleeping in while Kensy followed us with the diaper bag.

"Good morning, I'm Sabrina."

"Good morning," I said, trying my best to sound pleasant. "I'm Jack, this is Kensy, and this little one is Brayleigh."

"Nice to meet all of you. I'm going to get her vitals, and then Dr. Hughes will be in."

"Okay, thank you." I stepped back, let her do what she needed, and then tried to steady myself before Jane came in.

Brayleigh stayed asleep as Sabrina did what she needed, then left and closed the door behind her.

"Are you okay?" Kensy asked, sitting beside me.

"Yeah, just feeling a bit nervous this morning."

She reached over and squeezed my hand, instantly calming my nerves. We sat there watching Brayleigh sleep until there was a light knock on the door as Jane entered.

"Never in a million years did I ever expect to see you in one of these rooms," she teased, pulling me in for a hug as I stood to greet her.

"You're telling me," I laughed. "Jane, this is my girlfriend, Kensy. Kensy, this is Jane."

"We've met," Jane said, reaching past me to see Kensy. "But it's wonderful to see you again."

"You too."

"You guys know each other?" I asked, wondering if Kensy knew about my past with Jane.

"I did family photos for Jane a few weeks ago."

I rolled my eyes and nodded my head.

"That's right, I completely forgot about that. Sorry, I don't know where my head is this morning."

"I'm pretty sure I know," Jane said, looking down at Brayleigh.

"It was a rough night," I blurted out, feeling my cheeks flush as I admitted it.

"Babies have that tendency. Was she restless?" Jane asked, pulling the stool out from beneath the desk and taking a seat.

"She wouldn't sleep unless I held her. But then I was too afraid to fall asleep because I didn't want to risk something happening to her."

"Completely understandable. It's hard to balance your needs right now with hers. Did you try swaddling her?"

I frowned, unsure of what she was asking.

"Did I what her?"

"Swaddle," Jane laughed. "It's where you wrap her in a blanket and restrain her hands by her sides. It simulates the tightness she felt while in the womb while keeping her warm. Babies need that and she likely only slept while on your chest because it was warm, and she had the pressure of you holding her next to you."

"Oh, no, I didn't put anything around her. I know that it's not safe for her to sleep with blankets, so I wouldn't have thought about that."

"You can swaddle her during the day while you're there and monitor her to ensure the blankets don't come loose. But they also make wearable blankets that you can use instead that don't have any loose ends. You can get them in a variety of colors, thickness, you name it. I'll send you the link to some before you go. Try those and see if they help her sleep better."

"Okay, I'll do that." I relaxed some against the chair and reached for Kensy's hand. Her skin felt soft and warm against mine, which was instantly comforting.

Jane did Brayleigh's exam, which she decided to wake up for. She also showed us how to swaddle her with a blanket and different positions to try burping her. She laughed when I told her about the poop explosion this morning and said to get used to things coming out of both ends unexpectedly. We discussed the formula I had bought, and she agreed it was a good one to start with. There was a lot to take in, but she gave us some brochures summarizing everything so we didn't have to try to remember everything right now.

It was kind of weird to see someone I had a sexual history with holding my child that I didn't know about, but at the same time, there was no one in the world I trusted to take care of her more than Jane. Plus, it had been a few years since Jane and I had been together, so it wasn't like there was anything still there between us. She'd moved on and found someone, and I was focused on my relationship with Kensy. Jane was the best pediatrician in town, and I knew we were in good hands.

We finished, and I left with a list of more things I needed to buy, though this time, it didn't feel as stressful to go shopping. We headed to the store as a family of three, something I could see myself getting used to.

Thirty-Four
Kensy

Three days had passed with us trying to get into a routine with Brayleigh. I felt bad for taking a week off from work, but even worse when Jack's parents insisted on giving me PTO that I knew I hadn't quite accumulated yet. They insisted that *I* was doing *them* a favor by helping Jack figure out how to be a parent. It wasn't like I had any experience with kids, and honestly, he probably knew more from having two loving parents than I, who only had one.

We were finishing lunch when his phone buzzed. I grabbed it off the table and took it to him as he laid Brayleigh in her crib. Jane had been right about the swaddle sleepers—those things were a game changer, and we all were getting slightly better sleep thanks to them. We were still up every 3-4 hours to feed and change her, but at least we didn't have to constantly hold her while she slept.

"Thank you," he whispered as he followed me out of the bedroom and closed the door behind him. I went to the kitchen and turned on the monitor so we could hear her if she got up while he took the phone call outside.

I was looking through the fridge for dinner options when he came back inside. I closed it and studied his face, wondering what was going on. Given everything that had already happened in less than a week, I wasn't sure I could take much more.

"What's wrong?" I asked, pulling my shoulders back and taking a calming breath.

"That was my attorney calling. He got the results of the paternity test."

My heart pounded rapidly in my chest as I waited.

"I'm her father."

The breath I had been holding rushed past my lips.

"How do you feel about it?"

He shoved a hand through his hair and shrugged.

"I don't know. Relieved, I guess? I mean, I've already jumped into the deep end and have gone full speed with taking her in as my daughter. I don't know that I would have done anything differently if she wasn't, but it feels more reassuring that I've been doing the right thing now that I know."

"I get that," I said, stepping in front of him and wrapping my arms around his waist. "Did he say anything about the documents she left you?"

"Yeah, he looked them over and said that they're legit. If she comes back, she has no legal rights to Brayleigh."

"Do you think she will?"

"Will what?"

"Come back."

"I don't know. Unfortunately, I never got to know Zoe. It

was one night, and then suddenly, she showed up out of the blue, dropping off a child I didn't know about. She didn't even have the nerve to talk to me about it first."

"Will you let her see Brayleigh if she does?"

He shrugged and I felt him pull away.

"What's going on, Kensy?"

I frowned and took a few steps back myself.

"Nothing."

"No, something is going on. I can tell by the questions you're asking."

I turned and grabbed my iced tea from the counter, taking a long drink before I answered him.

"I don't know, Jack. I was just curious. I can't imagine having a baby and just walking away from it, so I guess I figured there would be a good chance she'll come back and want to be part of her life."

"You don't have to worry about that right now, Kensy. Let's just focus on the present and not worry about what may or may not happen in the future," he said, grabbing my hand and pulling me back into his arms.

"Okay," I said, but I couldn't shake the feeling that something big was headed our way.

Thirty-Five
Capshaw

It was amazing how much my family stepped in to help with Brayleigh when I went back to work. Thankfully, I was only on for 48 hours and then had 72 off, so it wasn't too much stress for us to all work our schedules around each other.

During the week, my mom or Lia took Brayleigh during the day, and then Kensy took her as soon as she got off work. If I was on shift during the weekend, Kensy took care of her, and my family helped watch her for a few hours so Kensy could keep up with her photography business. Originally she tried to step away from it and insisted that Brayleigh needed to come first, but we all insisted that getting her business off the ground was equally important.

I still couldn't believe that I had a daughter, but after the first few weeks, it felt natural and I finally felt like I was getting the hang of it. It was still hard constantly running on interrupted sleep, but I was making do.

My first shift back at work was stressful—not because we had any calls, but because I couldn't stop worrying about Brayleigh being away from me. I knew that my mother knew what she was doing and had raised Lia and me, but still, I was a nervous wreck.

The only thing I hadn't considered was how having a baby would impact my time with Kensy. Since Brayleigh came into our lives, we hadn't had sex once. My balls were blue every time I thought about Kensy and how much I missed being inside of her, but unfortunately, there was no predictability when it came to Brayleigh's sleep schedule. Whenever we started something, it was like she had spidey senses and would immediately wake up, essentially cock blocking me.

I wanted to take Kensy out and have some time alone, just the two of us, but I couldn't get past the thought of leaving Brayleigh with someone while I went off and had fun instead of taking care of my child.

"You're thinking way too hard," Nate said, interrupting my thoughts as he came into the living room and sat down. The firehouse was quiet as most of the guys slept, except Nate and I. I knew why I was up, but I didn't expect company at this hour.

"It's all I do these days. Think and obsess over things until I worry myself sick."

"Sounds like parenthood," he laughed. "What's weighing so heavily on your mind?"

"Everything," I sighed. "I miss how things were with Kensy before Brayleigh came into our lives, but I feel guilty for wanting alone time with her because I feel like it makes me a shitty parent for wanting time away from my baby. I love her—like a crazy fucking amount—but it's hard."

"Are you talking about how much you love Kensy or Brayleigh?"

"Both. In different ways, but I feel like I'm destined to fail one of them by not being able to be there for both of them the way they need me to be. On top of that, I feel like Kensy is pulling away, and that scares the shit out of me."

"Pulling away, how?"

"Emotionally. She keeps asking about what will happen if Zoe decides to come back and wants to be in Brayleigh's life."

"What did you tell her?"

"I told her that we would cross that bridge when we got there. I have no idea whether or not she'll come back. Her letter said that she wouldn't unless I wanted her to."

"Do you think you can trust her?"

"Fuck if I know." I leaned back, closed my eyes, and exhaled heavily. "Zoe was a one-night stand with someone I had never met before. We both agreed that it was a no-strings-attached hookup and didn't bother to find each other after that. I used a condom, so imagine my surprise when the paternity test came back confirming that Brayleigh was mine."

"Yeah, but condoms are only 98% effective. While they work most of the time, there's a reason they're not listed as 100%," he laughed.

"True. I guess I could have asked if she was on birth control, but I honestly didn't think it mattered. It wasn't like we knew each other or had any plans to get to know each other. She literally hiked her dress up in the bathroom stall at Surf 'N Shack and let me fuck her."

Nate chuckled and shook his head.

"Well, I'm sure your parents would be proud to know where their granddaughter was conceived," he joked.

"Right? But at this point, I can do no wrong since I gave them a grandchild. They thought they were going to have to wait on

Lia, but honestly, I'm kinda surprised that I was the one with the accidental pregnancy, given how boy-crazy she is."

"She's probably doubling up on birth control to make sure this doesn't happen to her."

"She better be," I laughed. "Med school has been making her grumpy as it is. Let's not add on hormones and a baby."

"So what are you going to do about Kensy? Do you think that maybe there's some jealousy about you having a baby with another woman?"

"I have no idea. I don't see why there would be, but then again, she did act differently after we left Brayleigh's appointment, and I mentioned that Jane and I had a past."

"You told her that you slept with Jane?"

I nodded.

"It wasn't my finest moment, but I felt guilty being in the same room with two women I had been with, and she didn't know. I explained that it had been years since Jane and I were together and that it wasn't really a relationship. Obviously, it was super short, and nothing came out of it."

Nate shook his head and ran a hand down his face.

"I thought it was bad trying to keep Jones from burning down the station every time he cooks, but you, my man, you need some serious help when it comes to women."

"No shit, Sherlock. I've never had a relationship get to this point, and now I'm fucking everything up. I'm 36 and have no idea how to be with someone."

"You've had a few serious relationships," Nate said, then

immediately retracted. "Well, somewhat serious."

"Like who?"

"The one who broke your heart and left you all mopey for weeks."

"Wanda?"

"I guess."

"The fact that you don't even know her name shows just how serious it was. And she didn't *break my heart.* I just thought we were on a different path than she did. I went on a mild sex binge shortly after that—hence my hook-up with Zoe."

"True. But there was that other girl, the one you brought to the Christmas party a few years ago. She even met your parents."

"Sasha. And she was a financial planner. She went to dinner with us because they needed to finalize their retirement plan that my dad ended up backing out of shortly after."

"Well, fuck."

"That's what I'm saying. See my track record? I'm already doomed, but the thing that sucks is that I really, really love Kensy. She's unlike anyone I've dated before. I can't explain it, but she's the one—I just know it. And now I might lose her because she's worried I'll let some girl I had one night of hot sex with back into my life."

"Tell her how much you love her, but maybe leave out the whole *hot sex with Zoe* part. That won't work in your favor."

"I tell her all the time, Nate. She hears me but doesn't believe me."

"That's the problem."

"What is?"

"You need to stop telling her and show her instead."

I inhaled sharply and thought about what he said.

"But how do I do that?"

"That, my friend, is something only you can figure out."

He got up and left as my mind started racing, trying to figure out how to show Kensy how much she meant to me.

Thirty-Six
Kensy

Things with Jack felt strained, and I didn't know whether it was the stress of him returning to work, having a baby, or all of the above. Either way, the one thing that really bothered me was how much I missed him and the way things were before everything happened. Don't get me wrong, I loved seeing him step into the role of being Brayleigh's dad, but I also missed the physical connection that had abruptly stopped between us. I knew there was just a lot going on right now and that things would get back to normal eventually—or at least I hoped they would.

It was slow for a Thursday at Surf 'N Shack, and I was ready to call it a day and go home. Since we didn't need two people up front working the register, I went to the back and helped Phil with some reports he was trying to get printed but the paper kept jamming.

Finally, we got it to work and I was sitting at the desk across from him when one of the bussers came in.

"Um, Kensy? There's someone up front asking to speak with you."

"Okay. Did they say who they were?"

He shook his head and then rushed out the door.

"Go ahead, I've got this," Phil said, nodding to the door.

I got up and headed up front, my stomach filled with butterflies not knowing who or what to expect.

The restaurant was still relatively empty except for a few tables occupied with customers and a handful of people standing off to the side waiting for to-go orders. I looked around and then found a woman sitting at a table by the window with her face turned away from me. I looked at Samuel, the busser, who nodded and then carried a stack of dishes to the kitchen.

I pulled my shoulders back, took a deep breath, and walked over.

"Hi, you asked to see me?"

The woman turned, and the second I saw her green almond-shaped eyes, my heart sank in my chest.

"Hello, Kensy."

"Mom?"

Her lips attempted to turn up into a smile, but the amount of Botox she had done limited the effort. I studied her face, barely recognizing her from the amount of work she had done to make herself look younger.

"Yes, dear." Her voice sounded strained as if it were hard for her to confirm that she was my mother. "Please, have a seat and join me for a minute."

"I'm at work. I can't just sit and chat."

"We need to talk," she insisted.

"About what?" I folded my arms over my chest protectively.

"Your father."

"What about him? He's been gone for six months, and you couldn't even bother coming to the funeral."

Her eyes narrowed at the tone I'd taken with her, but I couldn't give a flying fuck.

"I was on the road," she bit out. "I couldn't just drop everything and cancel my tour to be there."

"Just like you couldn't be there when I was growing up either, could you?"

She pulled her head back as if I had slapped her—which, honestly, I wanted to.

"Someday, when you have a career and kids, you'll understand that sacrifices have to be made."

"Are you fucking kidding me?" I laughed at the audacity she had to say that to my face.

"Do not take that language with me," she scolded.

"And why the hell not? You don't get to show up unannounced and start acting like a parent. You lost that privilege when you walked out on us!" I looked around at the eyes now on us and lowered my voice. "Whatever you're here for, I'm not interested. Go back to whatever hole you crawled out of and leave me alone."

I turned to walk away and stopped when she spoke again.

"I'm here about your father's life insurance."

I turned around and stared at her. *What the hell was she talking about?*

"What life insurance?"

"Your father and I took out life insurance policies a few years after we got married. I forgot about it until I got a notice in the mail from another company that wanted to sell me life insurance. Since you're set up as the beneficiary, I need you to contact them so they can pay out the claim."

My stomach churned as I realized the real reason she was here. She wanted me to collect the payout and give her money.

"Do you have the policy information with you?" I asked, trying to school my emotions.

"Yes, I have it right here." She reached into her oversized designer bag, pulled out a manilla folder, and handed it to me.

I opened it and thumbed through the first few pages as if I had any idea what I was looking for. Thankfully, it was rather simple and copies of the original application were right on top. Whether my dad made any amendments to this was unknown, but I was relieved that I was listed as the primary beneficiary and my mother as secondary.

"Thank you. I'll take care of this."

I tucked the papers back inside and held the envelope to my chest. I didn't know why my father never told me about this policy, but I still felt like a piece of him was attached to this, and I didn't want to let go.

"Do you want my phone number so you can call me when it's ready?"

"When what's ready?" I asked, furrowing my brow.

"Well, the money, of course."

"And why exactly would I be calling you about it?"

She pulled her head back in surprise, her neck looking rather uncomfortable as she did. *Dear Lord, how much work had she had done? It was like she was a walking, talking piece of plastic.*

"Because some of that belongs to me."

"How so?"

"I was married to him for over fifteen years," she scoffed.

"And you cheated on him for how many of those? Not only that, you weren't ever around—"

I was about to keep letting into her when Bella came in with Brayleigh. She spotted me and rushed over.

"Hey, I'm so sorry. I know you're still at work but my grandmother fell in the shower and she's at the hospital, so I have to get over there and make sure she's okay. Capshaw said to bring Brayleigh to you and that he'd talk to his mom about letting you off early."

"Yeah, it's no problem at all," I said, taking the car seat and diaper bag from her. "Call me later and let me know how your grandmother is doing."

She nodded and waved as she rushed out the door.

"You have a baby?" my mother asked, peering down at Brayleigh.

I turned the car seat around, blocking her view as I ignored the question.

"I need to get back to work. Thank you for bringing this.

I'll have an attorney look over the paperwork, and if anything is owed to you, they'll be in touch." I knew they wouldn't since I couldn't even afford an attorney, but it sounded like the smart thing to say.

"She's going to ruin your life," my mother blurted out as I started to walk away. "That baby, she's going to keep you from everything you ever wanted for yourself."

"Is that what you think of me?" I asked, biting my tongue to keep the tears from coming.

"Do you want my honest answer?" Her voice was void of emotion.

"Yes. I think you owe it to me."

"Fine," she sighed, tossing her jet-black dyed hair over her shoulder. "Yes. I know that sounds harsh, but had I not had a baby, my life would have been a lot different. Easier."

"Then why did you have me?"

"Because your father and I were having problems, and I thought that if I gave him what he wanted, he would give in and give me what I wanted. It seemed easy at the time, but unfortunately, my body didn't bounce back immediately, and I had to put some of my shows on hold. No one thinks a fat, pregnant woman is sexy. It derailed my career when I got pregnant with you. I was at my peak, venues were selling out, and we were finally where we needed to be. Then I got pregnant, and I tried to hide it for as long as I could. But once I started to show, fans reacted differently to me, and I knew I had to take a break until I could come back hotter than I was before."

I tried to take slow and steadying breaths, but her words cut me so deeply that I felt like I was going to bleed out from them.

"The fans reacted differently to you or the men?" I asked, earning another glare.

"Doesn't matter. None of that does anymore. I worked my butt off and got back to what they wanted from me, and I haven't looked back since."

"Obviously."

"Well, you seem *busy* with your hands full, so I'll let you go. Here's my number, be sure to have your attorney call me with the amount I'll be getting. If not, I'll be back to see you."

Brayleigh started crying as my mom walked off and left. I bent down and undid the buckles before pulling her out and holding her to my chest. This was too much. It was all way too much.

Thirty-Seven
Capshaw

By the time my shift was over, I couldn't wait to get out of there and go home. Bella had called me earlier to let me know that her grandma had been taken to the hospital and asked what she should do with Brayleigh. I asked her to take her to Kensy at work and then texted Kensy to give her a heads-up, but she never responded.

I called Surf 'N Shack to talk to her, but they told me she was talking to some woman who came in asking for her. I knew in my gut that something was wrong. It wasn't like Kensy not to reply or call back when they told her I had called. I rushed home to find her cuddled on the couch with a blanket wrapped around her even though it felt like a thousand degrees outside.

"Hey, what's wrong?" I asked, kneeling in front of her and placing my hand on her knee. Her face was red and swollen, her eyes bloodshot from crying.

"Brayleigh's asleep in her crib," she sobbed.

"And you're upset about that?"

"No," she hiccupped, wiping her tears away with the palm of her hand. "I didn't want you to worry that I wasn't taking care of her. The monitor is on, and I've been listening for her."

"I wasn't thinking that at all, Kensy. But what happened? Why are you crying?"

She covered her face in her hands and started crying harder, her whole body shaking.

"Shhh, baby, whatever it is, it's going to be okay."

I stood and scooped her into my arms before planting us both on the couch. She could cry all she wanted to, but I was going to hold her while she did.

"My mom came to see me today," she said softly. "At work."

"What?"

She nodded and kept crying.

"What did she want?"

She pulled away and sat up straight as she sucked in a lungful of air.

"She gave me paperwork for a life insurance policy that my father had. I'm listed as the beneficiary, so she wants me to file the claim and then give her some money once I have it."

My eyes bulged, my head shaking with disgust that her mother would even ask for such a thing.

"Are you fucking kidding me?"

"Nope."

"She expects that I'll have my attorney call her to let her know how much she'll get."

"Wow, she feels fucking entitled, doesn't she? I'm so sorry, Kensy. I can't imagine what you're feeling after seeing her."

"It wasn't just that," she breathed shakily.

"What else happened?"

Brayleigh started to cry on the monitor, pulling our attention to her. She was awake, which meant that I needed to go get her, but I also didn't want to make Kensy feel like what she was saying wasn't important.

"Nothing, I'm fine," she said, climbing off my lap and sliding over to the other side of the couch. "Go get Brayleigh."

I wanted to argue and tell her to keep going, but Brayleigh chose that moment to scream at the top of her lungs. Either way, I knew that I was letting one of them down, and that created more feelings of being a failure at this whole dad/ boyfriend game.

I rushed down the hall and picked her up, holding her against my chest as she calmed down. She was hot and sweaty, and from the feel of it, needed a new diaper. I laid her down and changed her, then went to the nursery to get a change of clothes for her so she didn't have to wear the gross, damp onesie anymore.

When I returned to the living room, Kensy was gone. On the coffee table was a note that said:

I need some air and time to think.

Thirty-Eight
Kensy

"Can I get another side of guacamole?" I asked, practically yelling so the guy could hear me over the music blasting around us. It was Thirsty Thursday at The Tipsy Taquito, which meant they had $3 shot specials of cheap tequila. I was already $9 in and ready to stuff my face with more green goodness, AKA guacamole, AKA the current love of my life.

"Should we cut her off?" Bella asked, pointing to my plate with a disgusted look.

"From the tequila shots or the guacamole?" Lia questioned. "You'll lose a limb or two if you get anywhere near her guacamole. And I don't know what's going on since she won't talk about it, but I wouldn't mess with her alcohol right now either."

They both watched me as if they were waiting for me to have some sort of mental breakdown—which, honestly, I probably needed. But for now, the tequila was numbing my head and keeping me from thinking about what a shit show of a day it was today.

I felt bad for walking out without giving Jack any heads up, but I also started to feel myself sinking even further into my depression and needed to get out of there. It felt like a wet blanket was sitting over my face, suffocating me. I had no idea where I was going, so I pulled out my phone and called the first person I could think of—Lia.

Since Lia and Bella had just moved into their new house, they were both there when I called. Within minutes, Bella was pulling up along the side of the road and told me to get in the car. We didn't talk, they just knew that I needed them right now and didn't ask questions. Apparently, they also knew that I needed food and a strong drink, so they brought me to The Tipsy Taquito and we'd been here ever since.

My phone had buzzed several times with text messages from Jack, checking to see if I was okay. Lia confiscated my phone before I could reply and hadn't given it back since. I knew he was worried, but I figured Lia told him I was with them when I saw her fingers fly across the screen before she sat it down and studied me.

A Backstreet Boys song started playing, and I swayed in the booth along with what I thought was the rhythm of the music until I saw the horrified looks on their faces from my lacking dance moves. I shoved another bite of taco into my mouth and wiped the excess guacamole off with my finger before licking it clean.

"Okay, now I'm starting to worry," Lia said, looking at Bella. "She HATES the Backstreet Boys, and yet she's attempting to dance to this song. Something is very wrong."

"Nothing is wrong," I lied, laughing as I popped a chip into my mouth and chewed. My stomach started hurting from how full I was getting, but I didn't let that stop me. "My mom showed up at work today and told me she regretted having me. No big deal."

I shrugged and kept bouncing in my seat though I wasn't sure there was a song playing at this point.

"Your mom what?" Lia shouted over the music, leaning forward so I could hear her.

"Yeah, she came by to tell me that my dad had a life insurance policy and she wanted money from it. Then she saw Brayleigh and told me I was ruining my life by having a baby. I asked if I had ruined hers and she said yes. She never wanted me, and I basically derailed her career. You should have seen the amount of work she's had done—I barely recognized her," I laughed, the hiccups from drinking too much now starting. "I mean, it's not like I would have easily recognized her anyway since she walked out when I was eleven, but I swear—she looked like a plastic Barbie. She was soooo stiff and rigid. It was like she had a stick stuck up her ass or something," I snorted. "All I could think was that I've never wanted to rip a Barbie's head off more than I did when I saw her."

I started laughing so hard that I had to set my chip down so I could wipe the tears from my eyes. Then I realized that I wasn't laughing anymore. I was crying and losing my shit in the middle of The Tipsy Taquito while my best friends stared at me with tears in their eyes.

I lowered my head to my hands and cried as they scrambled out of the booth to pull me out.

"No, I'm fine. Just let me be," I insisted. "It'll stop in a minute."

"You're not fine, Kensy," Lia said softly. "Nor should you be."

"Let's go home and talk about it," Bella offered. "I'll fix the guest room for you, and you can stay with us for however long you need."

"I don't want to mess it up," I sobbed.

"The guest room?" Bella asked, confused. "Trust me; you won't. And I'll make sure there are no socks on the doorknobs to scare you tonight. Lia can keep it in her pants for one night."

"No," I sighed, shaking my head. "I don't want to mess up Brayleigh's life. I don't know how to do this—any of this. I love her already and what if her mom comes back and I have to walk away from her? I'll be doing to her what my mom did to me."

"It's not the same, Kensy. I promise. Your mom chose to walk away. There was nothing that you did that made her do that—it's just who she is. And I'm sorry that you had such a shitty mom, but you're not going to be one to Brayleigh if that's what you decide you want to be." Lia squeezed my shoulder assuringly. "Now, let's go home. It's been a long day."

"Okay," I nodded and looked down at my plate. "But I want a to-go container for my guacamole."

"I'm on it," Bella assured me, hopping up and heading to the front to grab one.

Thirty-Nine
Capshaw

"Are you sure she's okay?" I asked, bouncing Brayleigh to try to get her to burp.

"She's fine. I promise. She's going to stay the night with Bella and me. Her phone is almost dead so I'm going to put it on my charger, but I'll have my phone on me if you need anything. I'll have her call you in the morning, okay?"

"Alright," I sighed heavily. "Thank you, Lia."

"No problem. She is *my* best friend, after all."

"Yeah, but she's *my* girlfriend. Or at least I hope she is. Fuck, I don't know."

"Calm down. No one is broken up. She just needed some air and time to think. A lot happened today with her mom, and she's processing all of it. Trust me when I say that this isn't easy for her. She has years of repressed feelings that she's being forced to deal with right now, and her mom told her some pretty shitty things. Just give her some time and let her have some space. Her world has been turned upside down since her dad died, and just when she thought she was getting back on her feet, all of this happened."

"I know. I'm sorry. I'm just so worried and want to be there for her. I hate that I can't be. I feel like I'm letting her down."

"No, Jack, you're giving her what she needs."

"You never call me Jack," I said with a grin.

"Yeah, well, I figured the situation called for it. Now get some sleep and give my niece lots of hugs and kisses from me. I'm coming by to steal her tomorrow since I don't have class and Mom needs to help at the restaurant."

"You do know that I'm off tomorrow, right?"

"Yeah, but I figured you need some time with Kensy, and I need some cuddles from my niece. I'll see you in the morning."

"You mean around 10 or 11, whenever you finally decide to get up?" I teased, knowing that Lia loved sleeping in when she could.

"You know it. Have a fresh pot of coffee ready, please. I'll bring the doughnuts."

"Deal."

"Good night, Jack."

"Good night, Lia. Thanks for taking care of my girl."

"No problem. Don't fuck it up when you talk to her tomorrow."

"I'll do my best."

I could hear her laughing as she hung up the phone. Brayleigh still hadn't burped, so I set my phone on the coffee table and sat on the couch, bouncing her on my knee as I held her chest against my hand. She was getting big so fast but she still felt so tiny to me. Finally, she burped, and her eyes fluttered closed as she started to drift off to sleep.

I cuddled her to my chest, gently patting her back until I heard soft snoring. Her nose had been congested the past few days, but Jane assured me that it was likely just mild allergies and she was fine since she didn't have a fever or any other signs of illness.

Once she was out, I laid her in her crib and changed into running shorts since it was too hot to wear sweats to bed. I wasn't tired, but I also didn't want to be up all night obsessing over things with Kensy. While I trusted that we weren't broken up, I still couldn't put it out of my mind that our relationship was in jeopardy right now. Things had been strained, and I couldn't blame her if this had become too much for her. Hell, it was a lot for me, but I didn't have a choice in the matter—other than one I would never make.

While I never thought about becoming a father, now that I was, I couldn't think about anything other than caring for my daughter and being the best dad I could be. Things had changed quickly, but I knew without a shadow of a doubt that this was what I wanted. Holding her and feeling her tiny fingers wrap around mine was something that immediately shifted my focus and locked her into my heart forever.

I laid down and tried to get some sleep, knowing that Brayleigh would be up in a few hours for a bottle. I put my phone next to me on the bed so it wouldn't wake her up if Kensy decided to call or text me tonight. I figured she wouldn't, but it was hopeful thinking that maybe she might.

Forty
Kensy

I was surprised when I woke up this morning without a hangover, given how many shots of tequila I had last night. Thankfully, we stopped drinking before we left Tipsy Taquito—though I was the only one who was really partaking, to begin with. Bella was the designated driver, and Lia was too worried about me to allow herself to get drunk.

We stayed up late and talked about everything that had happened with my mom once I sobered up a bit. It turned out that sopapillas were the key to soaking up the alcohol for me, and I was thankful that Lia had requested two dozen to go. We didn't finish all of them, but I was pretty sure my ass was two sizes bigger this morning than yesterday.

While I wanted to take the time this morning to sit down and go through my text messages from Jack, I had to get moving, or I was going to be super late for work. I rushed to clean up the best I could and then searched for Lia.

"Hey, I hate to ask but can you give me a ride to work?" I asked, nearly panting from running through the house. "I'm already late."

"Good morning. Nice to see you too. How did you sleep?" She lifted her glass of orange juice and took a sip as if she had all the time in the world.

"Lia! I gotta go! Your parents are going to kill me for being late. Can you give me a ride or not?"

"Calm down," she laughed, setting her empty glass in the sink. "You're off today."

"No, I'm not. It's Friday, and I was supposed to be there," I glanced at my watch, "an hour ago."

"I spoke to my mom and told her you wouldn't be in today. You're fine."

"Why would you do that?" My hands planted on my hips as I stared at her.

"Because it's what friends do, Kensy. You're in no condition to go to work today. You know it, and I know it."

"What did you tell your mom about why I wasn't coming in?"

"I didn't have to tell her anything. She saw your mom leaving and guessed something was up. I didn't tell her any details as I figured it was up to you if you wanted to tell her. But Kensy, you're like family to us; she knows your history with your mom. She's concerned about you and wanted to give you some time off to handle everything."

I inhaled slowly through my nose and then released it through pursed lips.

"I don't even know where to start."

"That's okay." She pulled me in for a hug. "You don't have to do anything today. Just relax and hang out. I need to get going, and Bella is already at work, so you can have the house to yourself for a few hours. Watch a funny movie or play some music. Whatever you need. There's food in the fridge, just try not to overindulge in the guacamole—I'm kinda worried you might turn green and I'll mistake you for Shrek," she teased.

"Are you sure? I didn't mean to intrude and take over your new place."

"You're not, and yes, I'm sure. I'll be back around six or so. We can figure out dinner when I get home."

"Okay. Thank you, Lia."

"Anytime."

She left through the garage, and I looked around the house, trying to figure out what to do with myself now that I had the day off. Knowing that I couldn't do anything without some caffeine, I headed for the coffee pot and stared at it, trying to figure out all the buttons. I wasn't used to it, and after fifteen minutes, I gave up.

I decided to sit down and put something on the TV to watch, but nothing caught my attention as I flicked through the channels. I was so restless that I couldn't focus if I tried to. My stomach growled, and I felt bad for rummaging through their fridge and pantry when I didn't live there or contribute. They lived close to Main Street, so I could just walk over and find something for breakfast without it being too far.

I grabbed my keys, tossed my phone into my purse, and opened the door.

My heart leaped in my chest as I stared at Jack standing on the other side, hand lifted to ring the doorbell. I startled him as much as he surprised me, jumping back slightly.

"Sorry, I didn't expect the door to open," he laughed.

"I didn't expect you to be on the other side either," I

replied, feeling the grin on my face. My whole world could be crumbling around me, but just being near him was enough to make me smile.

"I brought breakfast and coffee," he said, holding up a to-go bag of food in one hand and a cardboard tray from my favorite coffee shop in the other. "Can I come in?"

"Sure." I nodded and stepped aside to let him in. "Umm, Lia isn't here."

I wasn't sure if he came to see his sister or me, and I didn't want to assume he was there for me.

"I know. She's at my house watching Brayleigh. She demanded some auntie-niece time and kicked me out."

"Oh." I grinned, thinking about Brayleigh and felt this strange pain when I realized how much I missed her when it hadn't even been 24 hours since I'd seen her.

"How is she?" I asked, chewing my nail nervously as he pulled the food out of the bag.

"Lia? Fine, I guess. Sassy and demanding as usual."

"No," I laughed. "Brayleigh. How is she?"

"She's good. We had a rough night last night, but she seems better this morning."

He handed me the iced caramel latte.

"Thank you."

We sat at the kitchen table, our food set in front of us.

"What was wrong with Brayleigh? Why was it such a rough night?"

He lifted his to-go cup to his lips, took a sip, then set it down.

"I don't know. She seemed overly restless and fussy. Nothing I did soothed her, so we spent most of the night cuddling because she needed sleep more than I did."

"I'm sorry," I breathed. "I didn't mean to just disappear on you last night."

"Don't apologize, Kensy. It's okay. I'm glad you took the time you needed and had Lia and Bella to take care of you. I'm sorry if things with Brayleigh and me have contributed to the stress you're dealing with. I'm also sorry I didn't ask before I showed up this morning. I understand if you need more time and distance, but I needed to see you, Kensy. Even if it was just for a few minutes while we ate breakfast together. I just needed to see for myself that you're okay."

"I am. I mean—I will be. I don't really know how I feel about anything right now."

He pressed his lips together and tried to smile, but I could see that he was struggling.

I reached across the table and squeezed his hand in mine.

"The only thing I'm 100% sure about is you and Brayleigh, Capshaw. I love both of you so much that it hurts to be away from you. I realized that last night when I wanted nothing more than to go home at three in the morning."

"You just called me Capshaw," he said with a grin that made his dimple shine.

I shrugged, feeling the blush creep across my face.

"Your family calls you that, so I thought maybe I should too. I mean, I know we're only dating, but I think of you as family. I guess I should have asked first, or maybe we should have talked about where this was goin—" I started to panic when he squeezed my hand and interrupted me.

"You are my family, Kensy, and I love that you called me Capshaw. I've dated a lot of women in my life, but none of them have ever compared to you. I knew right away that I was falling in love with you, and I haven't looked back since. I want a life with you and can't imagine ever being apart again. Last night was pure torture not being able to hold you and make sure you were okay."

"I'm sorry, I didn't mean to put you through all that. I didn't know what else to do. I felt like I was suffocating, and I panicked."

"I get it, baby. I do. And I will always support whatever you need. You can count on me, Kensy. I know you've been struggling to find your place after losing your dad, but you don't have to look any further because it's right here." He held his other hand over his heart. "You're my family, Kensy, and I'm yours. We're in this for the long run, and I promise you will never feel alone again for the rest of your life."

Tears stung my eyes, and I was surprised I could generate any, given how much I cried yesterday.

"I love you so much," I cried.

His chair scraped across the tile floor as he shoved it back and came around to hold me. I didn't care about eating at that point, I just wanted to feel Jack and have his arms around me.

We stood there holding each other for a few minutes until I tipped my head up and my mouth found his. One kiss was all it took to ignite the flame that seemed to constantly be burning between us.

My hands locked around his neck as my legs wrapped around his waist, desperate to be as close to him as possible. He gripped my ass, forcing a moan between my lips as he deepened the kiss.

"I've missed this, baby," he growled.

"Me too," I panted, rubbing myself against his jeans.

"I need to touch you. Taste you. Be inside of you."

"We have the house to ourselves for a few hours. Let's go to the guestroom."

He carried me down the hall and plopped me on the bed before closing the door.

"Wait!"

"What's wrong?" he asked, looking around.

"You have to put a white sock on the doorknob."

He frowned and waited.

"Trust me, just do it."

"I don't have a sock," he muttered, looking down at his flip-flops then over at my bare feet.

"Hold on!" I jumped up and ran down the hall to Lia's bedroom, then rushed back with one of her socks and put it on the doorknob. "Okay, we're good."

I wiggled my eyebrows and jumped back as Jack reached for me after locking the door.

It had been so long that neither of us was worried about being sensual and undressing each other—we needed to fuck, and we needed it now. He stripped his clothes off a few seconds before I could get mine off, all of them tossed into a pile on the floor.

His hands roamed over my body as our mouths fused together again. I laid down, pulling him on top of me and spreading my legs. I knew it wouldn't take much and that neither of us would last long, given how long it'd been since we'd had sex or gotten off.

I pushed his hand down, forcing it between my thighs as he chuckled in my ear before slipping a finger between my folds.

"Ahhh," I cried out. "That feels so fucking good."

"You're so wet for me, baby."

"I need you to fuck me and make me come."

"You got it, but I want to watch you as you come undone. Come ride me, baby. Let me see those tits bounce as you come on my cock."

God, I missed his dirty mouth.

He pulled his fingers out and got situated on the bed before I climbed on and hovered over him. He gripped the shaft, running his hands up and down it until I finally slid onto it.

"Fuck," he growled, closing his eyes.

"Eyes on me. You wanted to see me come, right?"

"You fucking bet. Ride me, baby. Milk my cock and make me cum."

I paused for a quick second and started lifting off of him.

"Shit, we don't have a condom," I said, hating that I didn't want to go through Lia's personal belongings to see if she did.

"I don't want to make you uncomfortable, but I'm fine with not using one if you are. I don't have any on me, and I really, really want to fuck you. I'm clean and get tested every three months."

"I'm clean, too," I said quickly. "Now fuck me."

He chewed his bottom lip before gripping my hips and pulling me down on his cock. I cried out, rolling my pebbled nipples between my fingers as he thrust up from beneath me. I leaned back against his legs and spread my legs so he could see himself sliding in and out of me.

Then when I knew I couldn't take anymore, I leaned forward and positioned myself so I could rub my clit against his cock as we fucked. Within seconds I felt the tingle in my spine right before the spasm took over, locking his dick in a vice grip as I came. His fingers dug into my skin as he came a few seconds later.

Forty-One
Capshaw

The next two weeks flew by as I helped Kensy navigate things with her father's life insurance policy. We talked to one of my uncles, who was an attorney. He gladly took the time to explain things and helped her file the claim. He also assured her there was no way her mother would get a single penny unless Kensy decided to give her something after receiving the funds once the claim was paid.

Her mom had shown up at her work a few times, trying every manipulation technique known to mankind until Kensy finally threatened to call the cops. I wasn't sure which got her to back down—knowing that her face would be plastered across social media as the town nuance or the look my mom gave her from across the room as she stared her down. Either way, it worked. Kensy had my uncle draw up a letter confirming that she would not receive anything from the life insurance policy and sent it via certified mail so she couldn't claim she didn't receive it later. After that, Kensy didn't hear from her mom again, though she assured me she was more than okay with it. That part of her life felt resolved, and she was ready to move on.

Kensy was back at my house, sleeping in my bed every night and helping me take care of Brayleigh. It felt like we were a family, and that changed something deep inside of me when I realized that it was exactly what I wanted after I thought Kensy was going to walk away. It's true what they say—you don't know what you have until it's gone, or in my case—until it needs a little space to think.

Since then, we'd been inseparable, and our bond had grown closer. Kensy and I talked about anything and everything, never leaving any secrets between us. It felt like life was finally letting the pieces fall into place the way they were supposed to. It wasn't that I wasn't destined to find love; I just needed to wait until it found me.

"Are you ready to go?" Kensy asked, leaning up to kiss my cheek before stealing Brayleigh from my arms.

"I am. Are you?"

She chewed her lower lip nervously and bounced the baby on her hip.

"I think so."

"Don't be nervous," I laughed, pulling my girls into me for a hug.

"It's a big step."

"I know."

I rubbed her back soothingly, feeling her inhale deeply before releasing it.

"What if I'm making a mistake? Maybe I should just put the money in savings, you know, for a rainy day?"

"Like today?" I asked, looking outside at the rain drizzling down the window.

"My dad loved rainy days and used to say that

thunderstorms soothed him. I can't tell you how many times I'd walk in and find him asleep on the couch, snoring like a grizzly bear, as the thunder rolled outside. He'd leave the windows cracked so he could smell the rain and hear the storm; he loved them so much."

"Then maybe it's a sign."

"A sign?"

"You just said yourself that maybe you should save the money you're getting from his life insurance for a rainy day. It's raining and your dad loved storms. Maybe this is a sign that he would want you to use some of the money to buy your very first house and go after your dreams."

Her shoulders rose and fell with another deep breath before Brayleigh laid her head on Kensy's chest and started closing her eyes.

"Do you think it is?"

"I don't know," I said, reaching over to take Brayleigh so I could get her in her car seat before she got too comfy on Kensy. "But I think you owe it to yourself to go look at the house. If you don't like it, you don't have to buy it. Simple as that."

"Okay. Let's do it."

I pulled her in for another kiss, loving the way her giggle vibrated against my mouth before I released her, dragging her down the hall into the garage before she could change her mind. I knew that Kensy wanted to plant roots and have a place of her own, but I also knew that she was afraid of actually doing it. We got Brayleigh buckled in and then headed to the address she had written down on a napkin after getting a call from my uncle, who happened to know the best realtor in town. I might have put a little bug in his ear about Kensy wanting to buy a house, knowing he would find a way to make it happen.

I pulled into the driveway, glancing at the beautiful tan house in front of us. The front yard was perfectly landscaped, with just a few shrubs spread out amongst the gravel that took up most of the front yard. This would be easy maintenance, which was a selling point for me.

We got out and went inside, greeted by Ken, the realtor Kensy had been speaking to. He gave us a quick rundown of the house and then stepped outside to take a phone call so we could look at it without him hovering over us.

The house was brand new, with a spacious floor plan that joined the living room and kitchen in one open, shared space. There were large windows that framed where the couch would go and a beautiful stone fireplace that would keep the house cozy during the winter. We walked through the rest of the house, Kensy taking note of the massive soaking tub in the master bathroom before we checked out the guest bedrooms.

There were four bedrooms total, with two full bathrooms and a half bath off the garage. Everything was organized and laid out in a way that felt comfortable and functional. We had gone through the two bedrooms that shared the Jack and Jill bathroom, then went to the last bedroom tucked into the corner of the house.

When we first walked in, Kensy gasped, and I immediately knew what had grabbed her attention. The room was big—bigger than the other two bedrooms—and had large windows that brought in so much natural light that you didn't need much else. It would also make the perfect studio for her boudoir photography.

"Oh my God," she whispered, covering her mouth with her hands as she walked around, taking in every inch of the room as her mind raced with thoughts of what she could do with it.

"This would make the perfect studio," I said, adjusting the carrier Brayleigh was in.

"Right? I was just thinking the same thing! I could put a bed there so the room would have plenty of light without it being directly on the client. Then I could divide the closet space so they have room to hang their outfits while utilizing the other half for props and linens. I could even put a little vanity over there and get some shots of them getting ready, like retro style!"

I grinned ear to ear, loving her enthusiasm as she spoke.

"I think it's perfect for all of that."

"Sorry, guys, that took longer than I expected. Did you have any questions for me about the house?" Ken asked, leaning against the doorframe, taking in Kensy's smile.

"I don't, but she might," I said, filling in the awkward silence when she failed to say anything.

"Sure, I'm all ears."

Kensy's face flushed with heat the way it always did right before she did something she was nervous about.

"I do have one question," she said nervously before turning to me.

I tilted my head, wondering if she wanted to talk to me privately, though she didn't say so. I didn't know if maybe she wanted to know how to make an offer on the house or if she was nervous about the price.

"Jack, I know that we haven't been dating that long and that you already have a house that Brayleigh is used to. But I was wondering…."

She looked from me to Ken and then back.

"Will you and Brayleigh move in with me?"

Forty-Two

Kensy

I felt my voice catch in my throat as I asked Jack to move in with me, praying that he wouldn't say no—though I wouldn't blame him if he did, given that he already had a house and wasn't looking for a new one.

My heart raced as I waited for his answer, not knowing how to read the sly grin spreading across his cheeks.

"We would love to," he said, rushing over to cup my face without squishing Brayleigh between us.

"I don't want to make you sell your house," I murmured as he pressed his lips to mine.

"You're not. I want to." He peppered my lips and face with kisses as he spoke. "I don't want to be away from you, Kensy, even if it's only five minutes. So if you love this house, then this is where we'll live. Nothing matters to me but being with my girls."

"Are you sure?"

"100%."

I giggled as he kissed me more, hoping we weren't making Ken uncomfortable with our PDA.

"But I have one condition," he said, stepping away and looking me in the eyes.

"Okay. What is it?"

"You allow me to pay for stuff."

I leaned closer and whispered in his ear.

"I don't think that's necessary. You know that my dad's life insurance was enough to pay for this place twice over."

"I know, but I'm not okay with letting you pay for everything. We buy this house as a couple, Kensy. All of the bills will be in both of our names. We can figure out the rest of the details later. But I am not doing this so you can pay for things for us."

"Okay," I sighed. "We'll figure out the small details after we buy our first house together!"

I didn't hear much after that, the sound of Jack's laugh filling the room was the only thing I wanted to focus on.

After we officially made an offer, we dropped Brayleigh off with Jack's parents and went out to a celebratory dinner at The Tipsy Taquito. I had expected it to be just us but was pleasantly surprised when Lia, Bella, and Jones were already waiting for us with a round of shots and a huge bowl of guacamole.

"To new beginnings," Lia said, lifting her shot glass.

We all lifted ours and clinked them before throwing the alcohol back and letting the liquid burn our throats. Since Brayleigh was having her first sleepover tonight, that meant we had a night to ourselves, which was rare to come by these days.

Everyone was talking and laughing, but all I could focus on was getting Jack home so I could do all of the things I'd wanted to do all day but couldn't. As if reading my mind, he reached over and rested his hand on my thigh.

"We'll get through dinner, and then we're out of here," he said, talking out of the side of his mouth without moving the rest of his face.

"Eat fast."

"Trust me, I would gladly skip dinner here just to get home so I can eat you instead."

"But there's guacamole," I whispered, pointing to the bowl in front of us.

"Exactly. *I love to smother my tacos in guacamole before I eat them.*"

"Stop being gross," Lia said, shuddering.

"We're not," I said a little too quickly as my blush called my bluff.

"Whatever. I know that stupid look on my brother's face."

"She's just mad about the whole *sock* incident," Bella laughed, wiggling her eyebrows at Jones as he lowered his eyebrows in confusion. "The rule is that you put a sock on your doorknob if you're doing *it*, so people know not to walk in on you."

"And that works?" he asked, locking eyes with Bella for the millionth time since we'd been there.

"Usually. But luckily for Lia, she didn't walk in on them doing it. She just found her sock in the guestroom that

Kensy had stayed the night in before they kissed and made up. And I'm guessing they made up pretty good if Kensy forgot to return the sock."

My cheeks burned bright red as I tried to distract myself with more guacamole.

Thankfully, Jack took the opportunity to circle the conversation back to the guest room at the new house and what we were planning to do with the boudoir studio. This grabbed Bella's attention since she was going to do another session with me once it was set up so I could build my portfolio. Lia jumped in and offered to do one as well, but Jack had said not over his dead body. I could tell that it was just their usual sibling bantering but knew that it was going to get to the point of obnoxiousness soon if Lia didn't stop throwing shots and put some food in her stomach.

Jack took that as our cue to leave and grabbed a to-go container for the rest of our guacamole. The ride home was the longest ten minutes in my life as he teased me mercilessly by fingering me under my skirt and making me ache for him to fuck me.

As soon as we got in the door, we stripped our clothes off and rushed to the bedroom. There was no time for foreplay this round; it would have to wait until later. I was on fire and needed him to fuck this ache out of me.

But before I could tell him all the dirty things I wanted him to do to me, he was spreading my legs and reaching for the container of guacamole that I never saw him bring in with us.

"What are you doing?" I giggled, watching him dip a finger inside to scoop some out.

"I told you, I'm going to smother my taco in guacamole before I eat it. Now lie down and let me enjoy my dinner."

I laid back and let him nudge my legs open with his shoulders before I felt his fingers touching my lips, spreading it all over them. We'd played with food plenty of times, so this was nothing new for us, though we'd never used guacamole before.

It didn't take long for Jack to eat me and the guacamole, flicking his tongue against my clit to get every last bit before he sent me over the edge with a mind-blowing orgasm. I never knew sex like this before I met him, but now I could never imagine anything else.

Before we did anything else, Jack got a wet washcloth and cleaned up our mess. I loved how gentle and caring he was, even when we were both on edge, desperate to fuck already. He tossed the washcloth to the floor and then climbed up my body as he stroked his cock before lining it up at my entrance.

I used to think that my favorite thing about sex with Jack was when he would first slide inside, but now I knew it was the way he locked eyes with me. We had hot, passionate sex as often as we could, but we'd gone from fucking to making love, and that was something that would forever hold a sacred place in my heart.

****

Want more Capshaw and Kensy? See how things are going in the new house here— (Hint, it's going to be spicy!)
https://BookHip.com/ZWRGWGJ

Ready to see what Jones is up to? Check out his story in Four-Ever Single! https://books2read.com/u/4j5jMX

Looking for more small-town romance but want a little suspense? The Haven Brook series is calling your name!
https://books2read.com/u/m2RJNR

Other Books By Samantha Baca

The Haven Brook Series
(small-town romantic suspense):
'Til Death Do Us Part (Haven Brook Book 1)
https://books2read.com/u/m2RJNR

The Cradle Will Fall (Haven Brook Book 2)
https://books2read.com/u/b6O0QE

The Ties That Bind (Haven Brook Book 3)
https://books2read.com/u/mqgoz8

A Very Haven Christmas (Haven Brook Book 4- Novella)
https://books2read.com/u/mvqGjj

Three Strikes, You're Gone (Haven Brook Book 5)
https://books2read.com/u/mvqL2z

The Dark Shadows Trilogy
(romantic suspense)
Five Steps Ahead (Dark Shadows Book 1)
https://books2read.com/u/38Q0gO

Ten Seconds Too Late (Dark Shadows Book 2)
https://books2read.com/u/3JRgVB

Against The Clock (Dark Shadows Book 3)
https://books2read.com/u/m2YwoR

The Stone Creek Series
(small-town- novellas)
Chocolate Covered Mistletoe (Stone Creek Book 1)
https://books2read.com/u/3LRk9N

Candy Coated Promises (Stone Creek Book 2)
https://books2read.com/u/mldP5Y

Pumpkin Spiced Possibilities (Stone Creek Book 3)
https://books2read.com/u/bojdwV

Beaumont Creek Series
(small town)
Just One Time (Beaumont Creek Book 1)
https://books2read.com/u/3G52zK

Second Chances (Beaumont Creek Book 2)
https://books2read.com/u/4Aj6Z0

Third Time's The Charm (Beaumont Creek Book 3)
https://books2read.com/u/b5lEyG

Four-ever Single (Beaumont Creek Book 4)
https://books2read.com/u/4j5jMX

Fifth Wheel (Beaumont Creek Book 5)
Preorder link coming soon

<u>Whiskey Mountain Series</u>
(small-town- novellas)

Something To Talk About
https://books2read.com/u/4X62ag

Something To Think About
https://books2read.com/u/3GWAan

Something To Believe In
https://books2read.com/u/3yVzgB

Something To Live For
Preorder link coming soon

<u>Sugarplum Falls Series</u>
<u>(Holiday Novellas- can be read as standalone)</u>

Blame It On The Mistletoe
https://books2read.com/u/bw1rqe
Blame It On The Eggnog
https://books2read.com/u/38PPY6

Blame It On The Candy Canes (coming 11/3/23)
https://books2read.com/u/31DNo7

Blame It On The Blizzard (coming 11/17/23)
https://books2read.com/u/b6z6XE

<u>Standalone Books</u>
One Last Wish
https://books2read.com/u/mqg7D9

Finding Love In Apartment 2C (novella)
https://books2read.com/u/bze9aZ

Cocky Counsel: A Hero Club Novel
https://books2read.com/u/31Kzkn

All Is Fair In Food And War (novella)
https://books2read.com/u/bp8qjX

<u>Holiday Books</u>
<u>(novellas)</u>
Snow Place To Go
https://books2read.com/u/4A560N
A Christmas Wish
https://books2read.com/u/4EKXpE
Holiday Hijinks
https://books2read.com/u/4DP6Ze

Acknowledgments

There are so many people who help make every book as fantastic as it is, and I truly couldn't do this without their help! From my alpha readers who give me guidance along the way, to my beta readers who get it once I'm done—you all play an essential role in all of this!

Azucena, Chelsea, and Amanda—thank you, ladies, for all your help and for giving me the feedback I needed to make this the best book I could! I appreciate you all so much!

Niki, Katy, Claire, and Jennifer—I have the best beta readers anyone could ask for! Thank you for volunteering to take this on and help me with a few extra sets of eyes on this book!

To my ARC team, how can I ever express my gratitude for everything you do?! Thank you for signing up for my books as soon as I have a title—you don't even care if it's a year out from the release date, you still want it, and I love that!

Thank you to the readers who preordered this the second it went up and to those who planned to devour it as soon as it was live. You make my heart happy and encourage me to keep writing these stories for you guys!

As always, a huge thank you to my family and friends for being such an amazing and incredible support system. From telling people about my books to giving me time to write, I value everything you do for me!

Have you guys seen how much I love and adore my husband? I think I've only put it in 23 other acknowledgments, but I'm going to add it in this one too! 24 books later and you're still my biggest fan and busting your butt to make my dreams come true. I couldn't imagine a better business partner than you, and maybe someday soon, I'll be able to retire you! I love you and thank you for not divorcing my crazy book self!

To my girls—I love you and hope that you chase after your dreams the way that I am! No dream is too big, my loves!

About the Author

Samantha lives in the southwest with her husband and two small children after abandoning her childhood dream of living in a cabin in Colorado when she found that she couldn't afford to live there and was deathly allergic to the woods. When she's not writing, she's usually spouting off sarcastic remarks while drinking wine out of a coffee mug to look like a functional adult while chasing down her toddlers. She enjoys spending time with her family, watching reruns of Friends, and the 24/7 flow of coffee that can be found in her veins. Be sure to follow her on social media for updates on what she's working on.

You can find her here:

Facebook: https://www.facebook.com/AuthorSamanthaBaca

Instagram: https://instagram.com/author_samantha_baca

Goodreads: http://www.goodreads.com/authorsamanthabaca

Facebook Reader Group:

https://www.facebook.com/groups/2945710968775398/

Webpage: https://authorsamanthabaca.wordpress.com

Newsletter: http://eepurl.com/g0NcSj

www.ingramcontent.com/pod-product-compliance
Lightning Source LLC
Chambersburg PA
CBHW022115310726
48972CB00007B/2048